TENNEY

in the
Key of Friendship

⭐ American Girl®

TENNEY
in the
Key of Friendship

by **Kellen Hertz**

Scholastic Inc.

Published by Scholastic Inc., *Publishers since 1920*. SCHOLASTIC and associated logos are trademarks and/or registered trademarks of Scholastic Inc.   .
The publisher does not have any control over and does not assume any responsibility for author or third-party websites or their content.

Cover illustration by Juliana Kolesova
Author photo credit, p. 181: Sonya Sones

© 2017 American Girl. All rights reserved. All American Girl marks, Tenney™, and Tenney Grant™ are trademarks of American Girl. Used under license by Scholastic Inc.

ISBN 978-1-338-11756-1

10 9 8 7 6 5 4 3 2 1   17 18 19 20 21

Printed in China 62 • First printing 2017

For Mom and Dad,
who taught me to sing my own song,
and for Katie, who was always there to listen to it

CONTENTS

STUDIO TIME

Chapter 1

"*Y*ou nervous, honey?" Mom asked me as our pickup rattled along the parkway toward downtown Nashville.

"No," I said. "Why?"

Mom glanced at my legs, which were jittering a mile a minute.

"I guess I'm just a little excited," I admitted, squeezing my knees together to stop them from bouncing. Anticipation coursed through me as my pulse hammered with a rock 'n' roll backbeat.

We were on our way to Shake Rag Studios, where my friend Portia Burns was recording her new album. I've been playing music since I was four and performed on stage dozens of times with Dad's band, the Tennessee Tri-Stars, but I'd never been inside a professional studio before. I'd always dreamed of recording my own music for an album someday. Now I couldn't wait to see what it was like.

Mom steered our truck down a side street. A few blocks away, I could make out the curving Music City Center building. With its sloped wood shape and lean, fret-like windows, it looks just like a giant guitar. Seeing it, a wave of joy washed over me. *I'm so lucky to live here,* I thought. If you love music the way I do, Nashville is the best town in the world.

Before long we pulled into the Shake Rag Studios parking lot. From the outside, it seemed like a plain old concrete building. The outline of a golden guitar on the front door was the only clue that something special was inside.

In the lobby, the receptionist perked up when Mom told her our names. "Tenney Grant, of course! Mr. Cale has been expecting you." She punched some numbers into her phone. "Zane?" she said, giving me a wink. "The Grants are here."

Zane Cale is the owner of Mockingbird Records. I met him a few months ago when I performed a song I'd written in a showcase at Nashville's famed

Bluebird Cafe. When he asked to meet with me after the show, I was a bundle of nerves, hoping he'd offer me a recording contract. He didn't, which was super disappointing, but then a few weeks later, he asked if he could become my manager and help me develop my music. I don't think I'd ever been more excited in my life than I was at that moment.

I was still smiling at the memory when Zane popped around the corner. His curly gray hair reminded me of a mad professor, but his brown eyes were as steady as a hound's. As always, he was dressed in a style totally his own; today he wore a purple velvet vest over a Hawaiian shirt, jeans, orange cowboy boots, and his trademark porkpie hat.

"Welcome!" he said, shaking Mom's hand. Then he turned to me and squeezed my shoulder. "Portia's excited you're here," he said.

I grinned. I had only known Portia for a few months, but I felt close to her. We'd been paired to work together when my class teamed up with the Lillian Street Senior Center to plan our school Jamboree. She had helped me improve the song I wrote for the Bluebird Cafe showcase. Still, it wasn't until we performed together at the Jamboree that I discovered that her stage name was *Patty Burns*, and that she's a legendary singer-songwriter who'd written one of my favorite songs. Going to a studio session was cool enough, but getting to watch Portia record a song was a "pinch me" kind of cool.

"Right this way!" Zane said as he set off down the hall. Mom and I had to scurry to keep up with his long legs. He stopped at a green metal door and opened it. We followed him into a dim room lined with audio equipment. It looked like the control room of a spaceship: Computer screens, buttons, levers, and dials were everywhere. I wished that my older brother, Mason, who loves music gear, could be here to see this.

Zane sat in front of the blinking control board, next to a guy in a baseball cap.

"This is Rob, our sound engineer," Zane said. Rob nodded hello, his fingers flying over the buttons and dials. Across from him, on the other side of a wide glass window, Portia sat inside the recording booth with her guitar, wearing giant headphones.

"How-dee, Miss Tennyson," she said into a
microphone.

"Hi!" I said. "Wait, can you hear me?"

Portia let out a gravelly laugh. "There are speakers
in here so we can communicate," she replied.

"Oh, right," I said, feeling my cheeks pink up.

"I'm glad you're here, Tenney," Portia said. "I'm
feeling a smidge nervous being back in the studio
for the first time since my stroke."

I nodded, remembering that Portia had been
anxious about performing at the Jamboree. The stroke
had temporarily paralyzed her chord hand, so for a
while, playing her guitar had been really hard for her.
But since then, she'd been practicing and exercising her
hand, and she'd recovered so well I sometimes forgot
she'd ever had trouble playing.

"You'll be amazing," I said, giving Portia a
thumbs-up.

"You ready to get started?" Zane asked. Portia
nodded and tweaked her guitar's tuning pegs.

Mom and I settled into a couch to watch. Rob
adjusted some faders up and down and clicked a
red button on his computer screen. Then he signaled

to Portia, and she jumped into a twangy guitar riff
that made my foot tap. At the end of the intro, she
leaned into a silver microphone and began to sing.

> *You say it's all over for me*
> *That I've lost what makes me myself*
> *I say I'm gonna go on*
> *With or without your help*

Portia's voice soared, her right hand nimbly
switching chords as her left picked out the verse's
accompaniment.

> *It's all right, I'm okay*
> *I'll come back laughin' all the way*
> *I'll stand up tall, I'll break away*
> *I'll play my guitar, come what may*
> *'Til I'm old and gray*
> *I'll sing my song out every day*

Beside me, my mom was totally focused on
Portia. Mom had collected all of Portia's albums
when she was a teenager. As fun as it was for me

to see Portia record, I realized for Mom it must feel like a dream.

"How'd that sound?" Portia asked Zane when she'd finished. I thought it had sounded flawless, but Zane fiddled with his ear pensively.

"I'd like to hear you hit 'come what may' harder," he said. "Really let it out, you know?"

Portia nodded. Rob cued up the recording, and she started the verse again. This time when she got to "come what may," her voice turned darker and stronger. It still sounded pretty, but there was an edge to it, too.

"Great!" Zane said after she finished the verse. "Let's do another take."

"Really?" I blurted out, confused. Rob chuckled.

"Sorry," I said to Zane, "I thought you said it was great."

"It was," Zane said, "but that doesn't mean we're done. Sometimes we do forty takes of a single verse before we get it just right."

Forty? I knew recording a song was a long process, but singing a verse forty times seemed crazy. What did Zane want to hear? Before I could ask,

Portia sat forward, ready to do another take. When she was finished, they did another take. And another! Each time, Zane, Rob, and Portia would listen to the playback and discuss what she'd do differently next time. They talked about tiny details, like how long Portia should sing a certain word, or where she should take a breath, and she'd try it again.

After a while, all those small changes added up, and the song I was hearing seemed to shift. I couldn't really say how it was different. I just knew it was better. Finally, on the fourteenth take of the first verse, Zane said, "We got it. Let's move on."

"I need some water," Portia said. "Tenney, can you bring me some?"

Zane handed me a water bottle, and I took it into the recording booth.

Portia gave me a squeeze. "What do you think of all this?" she asked, twisting open her bottle.

"It's definitely slow going," I admitted, "but it's interesting to hear how the song changes."

"Yup." Portia nodded. "Some songs come out right the first time you play them. Other times, you need to play a song over and over, add new stuff, and take out other stuff, before you find the song it was meant to be."

"Really?" I said, scrunching my nose. The idea of a song I'd written having to be changed a lot made me queasy.

Portia squinted at me, like she was trying to read my mind. "You can count on change—in life and in music—so you gotta be open to it," she said. "The important thing is, did you like the song? Tell the truth."

"Are you kidding? It's great!" I said.

Portia swept a hand through her silvery hair, looking pleased. "I wrote it right after the stroke," she confided. "I could barely hold a chord, and I was so darn mad. Sometimes, though, getting riled up is good for the music. It gives you something to focus on." She sipped her water, studying me. "How's your songwriting going, Miss T?"

"Okay," I said. Ever since the Jamboree, I'd been working on new material. Zane had suggested that I work on my songwriting with Portia once a week. I'd only been to her house a few times so far, but I had learned a lot.

"I might have a song or two ready to play for Zane this week," I said.

"Perfect!" Portia said. "I can't wait to hear the changes you've made."

I nodded, my heart doing a happy pirouette. I still almost couldn't believe that Zane and Portia liked my music enough to want to work with me. Maybe if my songs were good enough, someday I'd get to record my own album, too.

We heard Zane clear his throat through the speakers. "Sorry to interrupt, you two. But we've only got this studio for a few hours, and I'd like to get this track laid down today."

"Okay," I said. "Good luck, Portia. You've got this!"

She winked and put her headphones on again.

When I came back into the control booth, I asked Zane for directions to the restroom.

"Just follow the signs in the hallway," he said.

I made my way through a maze of corridors to the ladies' room. I couldn't help slowing down to look at the musical memorabilia lining the walls. A long row of framed gold records and platinum records gleamed between photos of famous musicians, album covers, and signed guitars. There was even a pair of original Patsy Cline concert tickets! Taking it all in, I felt like I was in a dream.

My eyes fell on a glossy poster of the singer Belle Starr standing in the middle of Broadway downtown, where all the honky-tonks are. Belle was holding a gleaming gold guitar with strings that looked like they were made of fuchsia neon lights. CITY MUSIC FESTIVAL! was splashed in shining gold letters across the top of the poster.

The City Music Festival was one of Nashville's biggest events. Every club in the city is booked with live music shows until midnight for a whole week in April. Nashville's most famous stages, like the Ryman Auditorium, the Grand Ole Opry, and the City Music Center, are packed with some of the biggest music stars in the world. When the City Music Festival is happening, it feels like all of Nashville is dancing.

Maybe someday I'll play at the festival, I thought. I drifted down the hall, picturing myself singing under hot stage lights in front of an endless crowd.

Suddenly, I realized that I hadn't been watching

where I was going. Identical metal doors lined the hall in both directions. I had no idea where I was.

"Great," I muttered. Looking around, I started back the way I thought I'd come from. I turned one corner, then another. Finally, I spotted a green door ahead. Relieved, I went over and yanked it open.

A wall of noise crashed into me. This was definitely not our studio. It looked more like a rehearsal room, its walls bare and lined with soundproof paneling. A boy not much older than me sat drumming on a giant kit in the center of the room. His sandy hair pointed in a million directions. The kick drum thumped as his freckly arms flailed, his drumsticks hitting the cymbals and snare drums with an intensity that gave me an instant headache.

The moment he saw me in the doorway, he dropped his drumsticks down and stared at me.

"Who are you?" he said.

"I'm Tenney," I said. "Who are you?"

"Logan," he said. He gave me an expectant look, as if he was waiting for me to say something else. When I didn't, he finally asked, "What are you doing here?"

"I'm visiting my friend Portia. She's recording a song for her new album," I said proudly.

"No, I meant what are you doing *here*? In my rehearsal space?" he asked impatiently.

"Oh," I said. "I got lost. I was looking for the studio where Portia's recording and—"

"Well, she's obviously not in here," Logan cut in.

I winced, surprised by his rudeness. My stomach clenched in a flustered knot. But before I could respond, I felt a hand on my shoulder.

"There you are!" Mom said, looking relieved. "Honey, let's go say our quick good-byes to Portia and Zane. We have to go so I can drop you at Jaya's and get back home in time to make dinner for Aubrey and Mason." She glanced at Logan with a smile. "Oh, Tenney, who's your new friend?"

I wanted to tell her that Logan was not my friend, but I didn't want to be impolite. "Um, nice to meet you, Logan," I said instead, even though it hadn't been nice at all.

"Yeah, sure," he said, and started pounding away on his drums again.

COUSIN MINA

Chapter 2

*T*wenty minutes after Mom dropped me off, Jaya and I stood in front of her kitchen stove, flipping pancakes and cooking scrambled eggs. Every few weeks we have a sleepover tradition: We watch movies, listen to music, and cook our favorite meal, "breakfast for dinner."

Jaya's mom worked on her laptop at the dinner table, in case we had a kitchen emergency. As we loaded up our plates, I told them all about my trip to the recording studio.

"When are you going to get to record something?" Jaya asked.

"Not for a while," I admitted. "I have to get better at songwriting."

"I don't know about that," Jaya's mom said. "You wrote 'Reach the Sky.' That's a beautiful song."

"Thanks, Mrs. Mitra," I said, feeling my cheeks flush pink.

"It's true," Jaya insisted. "You're so talented. I can't wait until we get to hear your songs on the radio!"

I beamed at her. It was my number one dream to become a professional singer-songwriter, and I knew that I had a long road ahead of me. But Jaya's confidence in me made me believe I could do anything I set my mind to.

We carried full plates to the kitchen table. I sat down next to Jaya's mom just as a chime rang out on her computer, signaling an incoming video call.

"Oh! It's my sister Aisha calling from Bangladesh!" said Mrs. Mitra.

"That's weird," said Jaya. "Isn't it six o'clock in the morning there?" She jumped up to see the computer as her mom clicked to accept the call.

After a moment, Aunt Aisha's face filled the screen. She looked tired, but happy to see her family. "Jaya, hello!" she said, a gentle smile spreading across her face.

"Hi, Auntie!" Jaya said, waving. "How's Mina?"

I perked up at Mina's name. I had met Jaya's cousin last summer when she came to Nashville to visit Jaya, and the three of us had been inseparable. She had shared her MP3 player with us, so I got to hear Bengali pop, rock, and folk songs. Mina even taught us how to sing my favorite one.

Mrs. Mitra gestured at Jaya's plate. "Sweetheart, eat your dinner before it gets cold. You can speak with Mina when you're done."

Jaya took her seat and quickly started cutting into her pancakes, listening as her mother spoke to Aunt Aisha in Bengali. Suddenly, she stopped eating and looked up with a concerned crease in her forehead.

"What's wrong?" I whispered.

Jaya frowned. "My aunt just told my mom that a really bad tropical storm blew through their town yesterday."

"Oh no," I said. "Is her family all right?"

"I think so," she answered quietly, listening as Aunt Aisha continued with her news. "But she says that many homes and buildings were destroyed."

"That's awful," I said.

Mrs. Mitra and her sister continued speaking in

COUSIN MINA

Bengali. Jaya listened quietly, picking at her pancake with her fork. Finally, we heard Aunt Aisha yell in English, "Mina? Would you like to speak with Jaya?"

Jaya and I jumped out of our seats and crowded in front of the computer.

Soon Mina appeared. Her tear-streaked face softened into a weak smile when she saw Jaya and me on her screen. "Jaya! Tenney! I've missed you!"

"We miss you, too," said Jaya. "I'm so sorry about what happened. Are you okay?"

"Yes," she said, nodding slowly. "But my school was badly damaged. Our headmaster says that the building is not safe for us to enter, and there's no money for repairs. If we can't raise the money by the end of the semester in June, our teachers might have to find work somewhere else. And then who knows when my school would reopen." Her chin quivered, and a single tear slid down her cheek.

"Oh, that's terrible!" I said. Last summer, Mina had talked all the time about how much she loved her all-girls school.

Wiping her face, Mina explained that she was worried that she and her classmates would fall behind in school if it didn't reopen soon. "We're just hoping that we can raise the money as soon as possible."

"How are you going to do that?" Jaya asked.

Mina sighed. "I don't know," she said. "The people in my town are spending their money on fixing their own houses and hospitals and roads. Some people have given money to the school, but the repairs are very expensive."

"I wish there was something we could do to help," I said, shaking my head.

"That's okay," Mina replied. "It helps just to know you care."

"Of course we care," Jaya said, and I nodded. I didn't know what else to say.

After a long pause, Mina perked up. "Hey, I know how much you guys loved learning that song I taught you last summer. Would you like to hear a new one?"

"Yes!" Jaya and I said in unison.

Mina grinned. "I've been practicing for a school concert that is supposed to happen next month. At least I can carry on with my music even if I can't go to school right now." She reached behind her, pulled out an unfamiliar stringed instrument, and cradled it between her knees, its wide neck leaning on her left shoulder. It looked like the sitar that my dad had for sale in his music shop, but its body was slimmer.

"What kind of instrument is that?" I asked Mina.

"It's called an *esraj*," she replied, running her bow over its strings while her other hand moved over the frets. It sounded a lot like a violin playing deep, minor tones.

She began playing an upbeat song that made Mrs. Mitra, Jaya, and me tap our feet. When it was over, we burst into applause.

"That was awesome," I said.

"I loved it," Jaya added. "I hope you get to per-form that at your school concert."

"Me, too," said Mina. "My favorite teacher, Miss Alimah, told me it's a song about hope. I keep playing it as a prayer to keep our teachers at the school and to reopen the building as soon as possible."

When she said that, my heart broke. "We're send-ing you good thoughts from Nashville," I told her.

Mina thanked me, and we said our good-byes.

Jaya put our plates in the dishwasher and then

sat down across from me at the kitchen table, resting her chin in her hand.

"Such terrible news about Mina's school," her mother said.

I nodded. "I just wish we could do more than send good thoughts."

Suddenly, Jaya's face lit up. "We could!" she said. "What if we raised some money ourselves to help rebuild the school? It would be girls helping girls across the world!"

"That's a great idea!" I said.

"It is," Jaya's mom said, standing up. "If you want, I can e-mail the school's director and find out how much money it would take to rebuild. Although I'll warn you, it might be more expensive than you think."

"That's okay," Jaya said stubbornly. "If Tenney and I work as a team, we could raise the money together. It'll be fun, right?"

"Definitely!" I agreed. Besides playing music, I couldn't imagine anything more fun and important than working on a good cause with my best friend.

NEW IDEAS

Chapter 3

J had a test on Monday, but as I pored over my
textbook for one last study session, I couldn't
shake the melody ringing in my head. Music's
always taking over my brain at odd moments, like
when I should be thinking about fractions. I pulled
my songwriting journal out of my backpack. When
I get an idea, I have to write it down fast, or it buzzes
around my brain like a mosquito. I'd just finished
writing out the chord progression in my notebook
when Jaya rushed up to me.

"Guess what!" she said. "My mom got a response
from the director of Mina's school in Bangladesh this
morning."

"Oh!" I said, stuffing my journal in my bag as
we started down the hall. "What did it say?"

"They need to replace part of the school's roof

and repair some water damage," said Jaya. "She said it'll cost about three thousand dollars."

"Wow," I said. Jaya's mom had said it would cost a lot, but three thousand dollars? The most money I'd ever raised was forty-six dollars for a jog-a-thon in third grade.

"I know it's a lot," Jaya chimed in, as if she were reading my mind. "We just need to find a good way to raise the money."

"What if you designed a poster?" I thought aloud. "We could make prints and sell copies, sort of like you did for the Jamboree."

Jaya's eyes glittered with excitement. She loves making art. "Great idea," she said. "But I'm not sure we can sell three thousand dollars' worth of posters. Besides, posters cost money to print."

"Right, I didn't think of that," I admitted.

"Could we persuade Zane to let you record a song as a fund-raiser?" Jaya said dreamily. "If it became a hit, you would become a star and the record would sell tons of copies. We'd make more than enough money to donate to the school."

For a second, I imagined myself traveling the

world, playing concerts, and raising money to fix all the world's problems. Then I came back to earth.

"Mina said that the school would close if they couldn't find the money to repair the building by the end of next month," I said. "That means we only have about a month and a half. I think recording a song and waiting for it to get big would take too long."

"Good point," Jaya said, sighing. Her forehead furrowed with worry as we reached Ms. Carter's classroom and went inside.

"Don't worry," I said. "We'll figure out how to raise the money."

"What are you raising money for?" said a familiar voice behind me.

Our classmate Holliday Hayes stood in the doorway behind us, her golden-brown ponytail cascading perfectly over her shoulder like a shampoo commercial. I noticed that the colorful embroidery on her jeans coordinated perfectly with her jewel-toned backpack.

"Oh. Hi, Holliday," I said, smiling to cover up the edge in my voice. I've always felt a little uneasy around Holliday because she likes to make everything a competition—and she usually wins.

Jaya didn't seem to notice my discomfort, though. She explained to Holliday that we were trying to raise money for her cousin's school in Bangladesh. "But Tenney and I have to find a solution fast. The longer we wait, the more likely it is that the school will never reopen."

"I'd love to help!" said Holliday, practically sparkling with excitement.

I wanted to say that we didn't ask for her help, but instead I nodded politely. I remembered how she'd pretty much taken control of planning the Jamboree. I could only imagine how she'd boss us around about this!

Jaya seemed to be reading my mind. "Thanks, Holliday," she said. "Once Tenney and I figure out a plan, we'll let you know if there's anything you can do to help out."

Holliday's eyebrows shot up in surprise. "Oh," she replied, sounding a little hurt. For a moment I felt bad for her . . . but then she opened her mouth again. "You should. I wouldn't want to watch you two crash and burn just because you don't have enough help."

A spike of anger hit my stomach, but before I could figure out a snappy comeback, the bell rang and Ms. Carter asked us all to take our seats.

Jaya leaned into me playfully. "Don't worry about Holliday," she said. "I'm just glad we're doing this together."

"Me, too," I said, nudging her back so she knew that I really meant it.

That afternoon, Jaya told me she'd volunteered to help Ms. Carter take down winter decorations and put up spring ones, so we wouldn't get a chance to brainstorm fund-raising ideas after school.

"I promise to call you tonight," said Jaya, squeezing my hand as we walked out of the building.

"Sounds good!" I said. Spotting my brother waiting for me by the front steps, I waved good-bye to Jaya.

As I stepped down to the sidewalk, Holliday rushed past me, her backpack brushing my shoulder. She opened the door of a white SUV waiting in front of the school and glanced over her shoulder at me, crinkling her nose. I couldn't tell whether she was giving me a mean look or if she had to sneeze. Before I could figure it out, she flipped her perfect hair and climbed into the car.

"What was that about?" asked Mason.

"Nothing," I said, swallowing the hard pebble of irritation that had risen in my throat. Mason shrugged, and we continued walking the few blocks from Magnolia Hills Middle School to Dad's instrument shop, Grant's Music and Collectibles.

Dad gave us a wave when we walked in. He was on a stepladder, dusting the rows of guitars, banjos, and mandolins hanging along the far wall up to the ceiling. Every inch of the shop was packed with stuff: instruments, sheet music, vinyl records, and music posters. There was a rehearsal stage up front and a listening room in back. It was pretty much musicians' heaven.

My sister, Aubrey, came out of the back storeroom with our pet golden retriever, Waylon, trailing behind her. Aubrey was wearing one of her countless flower crowns. So was Waylon. Aubrey's seven

and thinks everything looks better with glitter
and petals, even if it slobbers.

"Finally!" Aubrey said to me. "Come play
hide-and-seek with me and Waylon."

"I can't," I said, pulling the tiara off Waylon's
head. "I'm supposed to play my new songs for Zane
tomorrow, and I have to practice."

"Nooo!" Aubrey moaned, like the world was
ending. "All you do anymore is write songs, practice
your guitar, and ignore me."

"I'll play with you as soon as we get home,"
I promised.

I grabbed my guitar case from behind the front
register and headed to the small, wood-lined listening room at the back of the store. I closed the door and
began tuning my guitar, admiring the white flowers
and birds inlaid on its aquamarine body.

Then I set my songwriting journal on the music
stand in front of me. Flipping through the pages, I
paused, looking at my notes for "Reach the Sky," the
song I had performed at the Bluebird Cafe showcase.
I had written it for my mom, because I wanted her
to know how much she inspired my music. It was

the first "real" song I ever wrote—all the songs I'd come up with before then were about silly things, like going on vacation or the time Waylon escaped from our backyard. But Portia once told me, "A good song is always about something meaningful to you."

I flipped ahead to my notes on the guitar riff I'd had in my head this morning. Hugging my guitar close, I strummed out the chord progression. It was a sad, slow melody, and I liked it a lot. But what should it be about? I asked myself.

I tried to think about the things that made me sad. Rainy days and math tests made me sad, but I didn't think I could write a meaningful song about puddles or long division. Seeing Mina upset made me sad, but I knew she'd be super happy when Jaya and I figured out how to raise the money to save her school.

Then I thought of Holliday and the way she made me feel this afternoon.

She'd made me feel the same way a few months ago, right after she found out I was performing at the Bluebird Cafe. "You're nothing special," she had told me. "I'm sure your music won't be, either." Even though it had been a while since that happened, her hurtful words still stung. Jaya and I definitely didn't need Holliday's bad energy around our fund-raiser.

Angry heat rose in my throat, and suddenly, the first words to the song popped into my head. I folded my legs under my guitar, took a breath, and started playing.

When it was time to go home, I had come up with the first verse and the chorus to my new song. *I guess Portia was right,* I thought as I packed up my guitar. *Some songs do come out right the first time you play them.* I couldn't wait to play my new song for Portia and Zane the next afternoon.

A BIG OPPORTUNITY

Chapter 4

*T*he next day after school, Mom drove me down to Music Row so I could play my new songs for Zane at the Mockingbird Records office. Most record companies have offices in big metal buildings with tinted windows, but Mockingbird is a small independent label. Its offices are in a cheery-looking brick Victorian row house. I'd been there a few times before, but seeing it still made me fizzy with excitement.

Zane greeted me at the door and guided us into his office, where Portia was waiting with Zane's niece, Ellie Cale. Ellie's job title was A&R coordinator for Mockingbird Records; that stood for "artists and repertoire," and one of her responsibilities was to be sort of a talent scout for the label. Ellie waved hello, and I smiled, remembering the day that she had handed me her business card after hearing me sing at Dad's shop. That day had felt like the beginning of the rest of my life, and in a way, it was. Now I was here, about to play my new songs for Ellie, Zane, and Portia.

The adults talked while I settled into the leather couch and started tuning up. As I tested the strings, I let my eyes explore the walls, which were decorated with unusual musical instruments. In one corner, an Australian didgeridoo leaned next to a Korean drum and a Moroccan oud. Last time I was here, Zane had shown me how to play chords on the oud, which was kind of like a lute.

I smiled when I recognized an *esraj* a lot like Mina's suspended over Zane's vinyl collection; it reminded me that Jaya was going to call tonight to talk about our fund-raising project. I had been playing with Aubrey in the backyard when Jaya had called last night. When I called her back, her mom said she was busy with homework, so we had agreed to try again tonight.

Zane's voice snapped me back to the present. "Ready when you are, Tenney," he said, pushing his porkpie hat back on his head.

"Oh, right," I said, feeling a nervous flutter in my chest now that I was about to share my songs with Zane. I traced my finger around the tiny mother-of-pearl songbird inlay on my guitar, a little ritual I've developed to help me calm down. As soon as I started playing, I felt more relaxed. The sound of my music made me feel like I was exactly where I wanted to be.

Over the next hour, I played two ballads that I'd been working on with Portia: "Good Morning, Glory," a sweet, pretty song, followed by "If You Come Home," which was slow and sad. I was relieved that Zane seemed to like both songs. He and Ellie and Portia took turns offering suggestions for a few minor improvements: a better rhyme, a stronger verse-to-chorus transition—nothing too scary.

"Is that all you've got for me?" he asked.

"Well, I started writing a new song last night," I said, perking up. "I really like it so far, but it's not totally worked out."

"That's okay," Portia said amiably. "Let's hear it."

I resettled myself and dove into my new song. As I sang, Portia sipped her tea and Zane stared off

A BIG OPPORTUNITY

into the distance. I threw my heart and soul into the chorus, but I only got to the first line in the second verse before Zane waved me to a stop.

"It's good," Ellie said, "but it needs something."

Zane nodded.

"Like what?" I asked.

"I can't say yet," Zane mused. "The melody's stronger than how you're playing it."

"What do you mean?" I asked.

Portia squinted, deep in thought. "I think what he's getting at is that your tempo is pretty slow, and this song was meant to be faster."

"But it's a ballad," I explained. "I like sad, slow songs because they're more emotional."

"Hmmm," Portia said, cocking her head. "Every good song is emotional in its own way. But the lyrics you've written aren't just sad—they're feisty, right?"

She picked up her guitar and shifted it onto her lap. Her arms twined around the polished instrument, and her hands found the strings. Then she started playing my song, note for note—Portia only needs to hear a song once before she can play it perfectly. She strummed the start of the chorus, fast. As she sang, her voice took on an edge. Suddenly, it didn't sound like my song anymore.

Zane nodded, pleased. "What do you think?" he asked.

"I like it better when it's slower," I said, uneasiness prickling my chest.

Portia studied me. "You know, your last two songs were this tempo and mood," she responded. "This song has a more complicated melody line. It might work better if you picked up the pace."

I shrugged, my mouth twisting into a stubborn knot.

"It doesn't hurt to try something new," Ellie said. "Try to open your mind about how you think about this song."

I nodded, but inside I was thinking, *I like my song fine how it is.* What if I changed the tempo, and the song turned into something I didn't like, or that didn't sound like me?

I thought about the story my mom had told me about when she'd signed with a studio and tried to make a demo record a long time ago, when she was just a few years older than I was now. The producer had wanted to change everything about her—even her hair color! She had told me that I should never feel pressure to make a change that I wasn't comfortable with. I wished she were here now to step in.

"What you have to remember, Tenney," Zane was explaining, "is that great songwriters don't limit their imaginations to one kind of song. They listen to different music and let it influence them to try new things."

"Like the Beatles," Ellie chimed in, mentioning one of my favorite bands. "Their songs show all kinds of emotions. John Lennon and Paul McCartney couldn't have written such different songs if they had been afraid to explore new sounds. Tenney, if you want to improve as a songwriter, you need to push yourself musically."

"I guess," I said, but my voice sounded as flat as a pancake.

"Remember," Zane pointed out, "the most important thing any singer-songwriter needs is a great set. Our goal for you this month is to build a solid, half-hour performance of original songs," he continued. "Each one should feel unique. They'll all be Tenney Grant songs, but they need to show different sides of you."

Electricity raced through me. I wanted to perform again more than anything else. "And you said that once my set is solid, I can start playing solo gigs, right?" I asked Zane.

"Absolutely," he said. "In fact, we need to get cracking, because I'm working on booking you for an upcoming performance."

My stomach did a cartwheel. "Really? Where? When?" I asked.

Zane tipped his hat off his head and bounced it on his knee, eyes sparkling.

"During the festival next month," he said.

"Next month? Wait . . . do you mean the City Music Festival?" I croaked. My breath caught in my throat as I envisioned myself performing on the Ryman Auditorium main stage.

Zane nodded. "At the start of every festival there's a welcome brunch for all the artists who will be performing at the festival. It's a chance for them to catch up with one another and get pumped about the week's festivities. Each year, a different label provides the entertainment. This year, it's Mockingbird's turn to choose. And I want you to play at the brunch."

"Oh," I said, realizing that Zane wasn't asking me to play in an actual festival concert.

Zane raised an amused eyebrow at me. "You were thinking I got you a concert slot?" he asked with a chuckle. "Sorry, the festival only asks artists who have albums out to perform at the festival itself. The good news is, along with the festival performers, everyone who's anyone in music in Nashville will be at that brunch. Playing for music industry insiders is exactly what you need right now: to get people excited about working with you."

I nodded, my brain filling up with possibilities. What if an artist I loved heard one of my songs and wanted to record it? Or even better, wanted me to sing it with them! Playing at the City Music Festival artists' brunch could easily lead to more musical opportunities.

"So you're interested?" Zane asked.

"Yes," I said, hugging my guitar. "I am definitely interested."

TENNEY

All during dinner that night, my mind kept floating up into dreamland as I imagined myself performing in front of a crowd of musicians whom I loved and admired. It was thrilling and terrifying at the same time. The City Music Festival was just five weeks away, I realized, counting the days. That wasn't a lot of time to get a flawless set of original songs together.

Waylon followed me upstairs and watched me finish my homework. Then I grabbed my guitar and my songwriting journal and sat on my bed to work on music. I started with my new song. At first I tried playing it faster and hardening my voice, but I didn't feel like myself—I just sounded like I was imitating somebody else. Portia, Ellie, and Zane had urged me to branch out to make my song more powerful. But how could I do that and stay true to my music? As I thought about it, my stomach felt topsy-turvy.

Calm down, I told myself. *You can do this.* I opened my journal and looked at the notes I had jotted down from our session. Feisty. Driving. Powerful. Faster. The words seemed to describe a rock 'n' roll song. *Maybe that's what everyone wants to hear,* I thought.

I played the song twice, trying to make the song sound "rock." The harder I tried, though, the more it just sounded rushed. I growled in frustration. I took a breath and started over, closing my eyes. Usually, that helps me hear the song better. This time, I changed keys to see if that would somehow make it sound more rock 'n' roll. It just sounded weird instead.

I sighed, exhaling my frustration. Then I tried one of the verses again in the original key.

> *It's always been just her and me*
> *We've no need for your thoughts*
> *There's no room for your bad energy*
> *We're giving it our best shot*

I listened to the words as I sang. They were strong and hurt and a little angry. Under them, my melody seemed too soft. *Maybe Portia was right,* I thought. It needs to be punchier. I started reworking the chorus melody.

TENNEY

Right when I felt like I was on the verge of a breakthrough, our home phone rang, and Mom picked up in the kitchen.

"Tenney! It's for you!" she called.

I left my guitar on the bed and grabbed the phone in the hallway, humming my new chorus.

"Hello?" I said into the receiver. The music I'd been working out was still playing in my head, so for a second I only heard every other word that Jaya was saying.

"—and I thought it would be a great idea!" she finished. She paused, waiting for me to respond.

Oops, I realized. I had no idea what she'd been talking about. "Sorry, Jaya," I said. "I'm a little distracted. Can you repeat that?"

"I want to put on a book drive to raise money for Mina's school in Bangladesh!" Jaya bubbled enthusiastically. "We'll collect used books and resell them at the Spring Clean!"

The Magnolia Hills Spring Clean happens every April. My classmates and their families donate used toys, clothes, appliances, and even bikes, and our school hosts a rummage sale one Saturday in the gym.

"Normally, all the money goes to after-school sports, but I already asked Ms. Carter if she could make an exception for books, and she's going to check!" Jaya continued.

"Okay," I said. I felt a little hurt that Jaya had already asked Ms. Carter to okay her idea. She hadn't even asked my opinion first.

"I guess a book drive could be good," I said. I wasn't too psyched about the idea, but Jaya sounded so excited that I decided to keep my opinion to myself.

"It'll be great!" Jaya replied. "We'll collect books at school and around the neighborhood for the next few weeks. Then we'll price them and sell them in a stall at the event. A million people come to the Spring Clean. We could sell out!"

I tried to get a word in edgewise, but Jaya was talking way too fast. As she chattered in my ear, the melody I'd just made up started to get fuzzy in my brain.

"Hey, Jaya?" I interrupted. "I have to go."

"Okay," said Jaya, surprise edging her voice.

"Great thinking, though. We'll talk about it more tomorrow," I said. I hung up the phone and hummed my new melody again to make sure I hadn't lost it. *Jaya will understand why I had to get off the phone,* I thought as I pulled my guitar back into my lap. *Right now, I need to focus on my music.*

TWO SURPRISES

Chapter 5

hen I walked into class the next morning, I spotted Jaya talking to Ms. Carter at her desk. Our teacher waved me over with a warm smile.

"Tenney!" she said. "I was just telling Jaya that I spoke with Principal Schreiber, and she's fine with you girls selling books at the Spring Clean to raise money for your project in Bangladesh!"

"That's great!" I said. I turned to Jaya to share my excitement, but she kept her eyes glued on Ms. Carter.

"We're both very impressed with the initiative y'all are showing," Ms. Carter continued. "Good luck!"

As we settled at our desks, more kids came in, and Ms. Carter wrote the morning lesson on the board. I waited for Jaya to turn around in her seat to chat. Instead, she kept her back to me.

"I'm glad that Ms. Carter is helping us make the book sale happen," I whispered to the back of Jaya's head.

Jaya nodded but didn't say anything.

She's in a funny mood, I thought. Maybe she just forgot to eat breakfast.

Throughout first period, Jaya remained facing the front of the classroom. When the bell rang at the end of class, Jaya stayed quiet as we spilled into the hallway with the rest of our classmates. I was about to ask if something was wrong when a blur of golden hair stepped between us.

"Hey!" said the blur, which turned out to be Holliday Hayes. "Good news: My dad said we can put donation boxes at his company offices."

"Fantastic!" Jaya said, beaming at Holliday.

I was confused. "Boxes for what?" I asked, doing a two-step to catch up to them.

"Collection boxes," said Holliday. "For the book drive."

"Oh?" I said, looking to Jaya for an explanation.

Jaya finally looked at me for the first time this morning. "After you couldn't talk last night,

TWO SURPRISES

I wanted to get another opinion, so I called Holliday
and told her about my idea—"

"And I was happy to help out!" Holliday said,
finishing Jaya's sentence. They both laughed.

I swallowed hard. *So that's why Jaya is upset,*
I realized. *Because I was distracted last night.* I'd have to
explain to her later, when it was just the two of us.

"I also thought we could post flyers around
town," Holliday continued. "And ask local businesses
to put out more donation boxes!"

"Good idea," Jaya said, her eyes twinkling as she
beamed at Holliday. "You're going to be a great part
of the team!"

"I agree!" Holliday said, with a satisfied skip.

I smiled politely. *Maybe Jaya's right about Holliday,*
I thought as I walked with the two of them. Holliday
was really organized. She had headed up the sixth
grade's Jamboree planning committee, after all.

Still, Holliday had a mean streak. Why would
Jaya want to get her involved in our project? And
why didn't Jaya ask me if I wanted to work with
Holliday? I'd assumed raising money for Mina's
school was going to be something Jaya and I were

going to accomplish together. Finding out that she'd
turned to Holliday made me feel a little less special,
but I tried not to let it bother me. *The important thing
is that we're all working together for a good cause,* I told
myself. *That's what I need to focus on.*

At lunch, the three of us sat down with our
cafeteria pizza and worked out the details of the
book drive.

"I liked Holliday's idea to put donation boxes in
the school and around the neighborhood," Jaya said,
"but where do we get the boxes?"

"My dad has lots of old shipping boxes at his
store," I said. "We can use some of those. I bet we
can set up a donation box there, too, and at the senior
center, the grocery store, and the library. We can send
out a schoolwide e-mail."

"And put up the flyers Holliday suggested," Jaya
reminded me as she took notes. She looked up and
gave me a warm smile. I felt like things were finally
starting to get back to normal between us.

"What about morning announcements?"
Holliday suggested, tucking a lock of golden hair
behind her ear. "I can do an all-school intercom

announcement every Monday to remind people to bring in their old books."

"Good idea," I said.

Holliday beamed at me. Surprised, I gave her a cautious smile back. Maybe working with Holliday wouldn't be so bad after all.

"We should get together after school to keep planning," Jaya suggested. "I have art club after school today, but what about tomorrow?"

"I'm free," said Holliday.

"I can't tomorrow," I said. I had promised Portia and Zane that we'd start meeting three times a week to polish my songs for the City Music Festival brunch. "But I could meet the next day . . ."

Jaya's face fell. "Tenney, we need to get started on this right away," she told me, sounding like a teacher. "We only have a few weeks until the Spring Clean."

"I know, but I can't miss my songwriting session," I said.

We sat there in awkward silence until Holliday jumped in. "Why don't Jaya and I meet tomorrow," she said to me. "Then we'll text you where we're going to put the boxes, and we can figure out a good time to put up flyers and stuff."

"Yes!" Jaya said.

My heart sank a little. I wished that Jaya had wanted to wait until all three of us could meet in person, but I felt like I couldn't really complain. Instead, I just nodded and hoped I could make it up to Jaya sometime this week.

When school let out the next day, I wished Jaya and Holliday luck with project planning and headed to the front steps to meet my mom. She wasn't hard to find among the minivans and yellow school buses picking up my classmates. I grinned at the sight of Mom's robin's-egg-blue food truck in the parking lot, with GEORGIA'S GENUINE TENNESSEE HOT CHICKEN scrolled across the side in tomato-red letters. I hopped in, and Mom turned out of the parking lot. We were headed for Shake Rag Studios, where Portia was still recording her album. Zane had suggested we meet there.

TWO SURPRISES

As we pulled into the driveway of the studio, Mom kissed me on the forehead and wished me luck.

My stomach got queasy as I thought about playing the new, "rock" version of my song for Portia and Zane. "I wish you could come in with me," I said.

Mom gave me a regretful smile.

"Me, too, honey," she said, "but I have to pick up some extra supplies for my event tonight. I'll meet you back here at four thirty, okay? Text me if there's a problem."

I nodded but didn't budge.

"Don't be nervous," Mom said, reading my mind as usual. "You'll do great."

I gave her a big hug, trying to believe her.

Inside, the receptionist walked me down the hall to a rehearsal room that was much larger than the one where I'd met that rude drummer, Logan. Portia and Zane stood talking next to a baby grand piano. A full drum kit stood nearby.

"How's it going?" Zane asked, as Portia gave me a squeeze.

"Good," I said, although my heart was beating double time.

Zane got me a bottle of water as I unsnapped my case and took out my guitar. Zane and Portia waited while I sat on a stool and warmed up.

"What do you say we work on your newest tune first?" Zane asked.

I nodded reluctantly.

Portia raised an eyebrow. "Okay," she said. "Are you ready?"

Not really, I almost said, but it was now or never. Digging my fingers into my guitar frets, I took a deep breath and attacked the song. My new tempo for the song was faster—much faster, I realized as my brain spun. Every chord I played sounded too loud and abrupt, but I kept going, stumbling through the new chorus and the bridge with my eyes glued to the frets. The last verse was a blur of mumbled lyrics and messy guitar licks. It all felt weird and wrong.

When I looked at Zane and Portia after the song ended, I could tell they felt the same way.

"It's bad," I said, hopelessness drowning my voice.

"Come on, now," Zane said mildly. "It's rough, that's all."

TWO SURPRISES

I shook my head. "That melody just isn't a rock melody."

"I don't think that's the problem," Portia said softly.

Surprise shot through me, and I looked at Portia. Her expression was gentle, but her blue eyes were sharp.

"The problem," she said, "is that you didn't really change the song, Tenney. You shifted a few notes in the chorus, and you sped it up, but you didn't rethink the song."

"I—I tried," I stammered, my cheeks growing hot with embarrassment. "If you don't like it, maybe it's because the song doesn't need changes."

Portia and Zane exchanged a look. I could tell they weren't buying it.

"I know how you might be able to start hearing what's missing," Zane said good-naturedly. He left the room and returned a minute later, a big grin stretching across his face. "I'd like you to meet a friend of mine," he said as a figure appeared in the doorway behind him. "This is Logan Everett."

Logan stepped into the room. I blinked hard

to make sure I wasn't seeing things.

His eyes locked on me. "Oh. Hi . . ." he said, trailing off.

I realized he didn't remember my name.

"Tenney," I said stiffly.

"Right," Logan said.

"You two know each other?" said Zane, perking up. "That's great!" He pushed his hat back on his head and leaned forward.

"Logan's got great instincts as a drummer," Zane continued. "After I heard this song the first time, Tenney, I brainstormed what could make it even better. I thought, why don't we invite Logan in for a jam session and see what happens?"

"Oh!" I said a little too loudly, trying to disguise the disappointment in my voice. Zane didn't seem to notice.

"I think your sounds will really complement each other," he said enthusiastically. "If this goes well, I'm thinking you two could play together at the City Music Festival artists' brunch."

It was as if someone had plunged my heart into ice water.

TWO SURPRISES

"Play together?" I croaked.

Zane gave me a nod and a broad smile.

I shot a glance at Logan. Sagging in the corner, he looked about as frustrated as I felt.

There was no way in a million years that I wanted to play music with Logan Everett. But right now, it looked like something I couldn't avoid.

IN A JAM

Chapter 6

I can't believe this is happening, I thought, as Logan settled in behind the drum kit. Suddenly, I deeply regretted skipping Jaya's project-planning meeting to come to the studio. For a moment, I considered faking a stomachache or playing terribly to make it sound like Logan and I were an awful match—anything to get out of that room as soon as possible! But then I realized that Zane might wonder whether I was ready to perform at the City Music Festival brunch, and I couldn't risk losing his trust in me.

I swallowed hard and slung my guitar across my shoulders. Anger, fear, and worry stormed inside me, and I felt like I could bubble over into tears.

Portia sat down next to me. "You okay?" she asked softly.

"Not really," I muttered.

She leaned down, forcing me to meet her gaze.

"I know this is confusing, but nothing's set in stone," she said. "Just focus on the music, okay? Remember, this is an opportunity for you to grow as a songwriter."

I nodded halfheartedly. Normally, I love jamming with anyone, especially when we're playing one of my songs. My family even has a Sunday tradition where we play all the tunes that we love. But I didn't trust Logan.

I glanced over to where he was warming up— loudly. It sounded less like drumming than a never-ending car crash. My head started to throb as Zane waved him to a stop.

"Okay, let's get going," Zane said. "Tenney, play your song the way you originally wrote it. Keep it simple. Logan, you listen, think about how you could back her, and if you feel like you can join in, bring the tempo up, and give it an edge."

Logan nodded, twirling his drumsticks in both hands like he was showing off. It was really annoying.

Zane glanced at me. Taking a deep breath, I started my song. I played slowly, trying to draw attention to the beauty of the melody. *Listen,* I tried to say through the music, *this song doesn't need to be faster. It's perfect how it is. Listen.*

I'd barely finished the first verse when Logan's voice broke into the song.

"It's pretty sleepy," he said.

I paused, annoyance prickling down my back. *"Sleepy?"* I repeated.

Logan nodded, giving a yawn the size of Texas.

"You haven't even heard the whole song yet," I said sharply.

Logan shrugged. "I can tell where it's going," he said. The fact that he was so casual made me even more frustrated.

Before I could figure out a snappy comeback, though, Portia stood up. "We should leave you two alone," she said.

I felt panicked, like a fish caught in a net. "What? Why?" I burst out.

"So you can work it out together," Portia replied. "We're just going into the control booth. We'll watch from there."

Zane nodded. "We'll be able to hear and see

everything. We'll chime in if we have suggestions, but I want the two of you to work on the song like we're not here, okay?"

"No problem," Logan said, stretching behind his cymbal stands.

This was not how I thought things were going to go. Still, I didn't want Logan to see that I was rattled.

"That's fine," I said, holding my chin up.

"Great," Portia said, squeezing my shoulder.

She and Zane exited through a side door. After a moment, they appeared in an upper window that looked into the rehearsal room.

"Whenever you're ready," Zane said, through the intercom.

"I'll set the beat, and you follow," Logan told me. Before I could reply, he launched into a brisk rock tempo.

"C'mon!" he shouted over the drums.

I felt like rolling my eyes, but my parents raised me better than that. Instead, I dug my fingers into my guitar frets, counted off a couple of measures in my head, and started playing. The beat was fast, but manageable. *I can do this,* I thought, relaxing.

Big mistake. As I exhaled, Logan changed the beat. Suddenly, he was playing triplets! It sounded like a runaway train. My fingers stuttered to an off-tempo halt.

"Why'd you stop?" Logan asked.

"You changed the beat," I shot back.

"I was experimenting," he told me, as if I was in preschool. "That's what you do when you jam."

"I know," I said, irritated, "but where I come from, you let people know before you change the beat."

"You need to roll with it," Logan said. "My dad taught me that when things change, you just keep going."

I felt like I had swallowed a flaming-hot pepper of fury, but I fought the urge to explode.

"A triplet beat confuses the melody," I said in a tight voice. "Can you play something else, please?"

Logan blinked at me for what felt like forever. "Whatever you want," he said finally.

"Good," I said. I turned my back to him and started over.

IN A JAM

This time, Logan kept pace with me for the first verse and the chorus. As soon as I hit the second verse, though, he started adding cymbal hits. I kept going, ignoring him and his cymbal crashes. It worked okay for a while, and I even improvised some new lyrics:

It was only going to be her and me
And then you came in with your thoughts
Planning everything so perfectly
Giving your best shot

But when we started the second chorus, Logan's backbeat was suddenly all wrong. He was out of time with my singing, and he didn't even try to adjust! We sounded horrible.

For a heartbeat, I thought about matching Logan's tempo. Then stubbornness knotted my jaw. *No way,* I thought. *He should match me.*

We slogged through the rest of the song. When it was over, I looked at Zane and Portia in the sound booth window. They were frowning.

"Guys, playing together means listening to

each other," Zane said through the intercom. "That was a mess."

"Well, Logan wasn't listening to me!" I protested.

"No! You didn't adjust to me!" Logan shouted over me.

"You're both right, and you're both wrong," Portia said calmly. "So, what are you going to do about it?"

I gritted my teeth and stared down at my guitar. "We need to work together and listen," I grumbled.

"Good idea. Do that," said Portia.

I glared at Logan. His cheeks were bright pink, but his eyes were serious. When I started the song over, Logan fell into a beat that matched my tempo.

At the end of the first verse, he picked up the beat slightly. I followed him, and when he added some heat to the chorus, so did I. For a measure or two, we sounded okay.

Then Logan started pounding on the drums.

Annoyance burned inside me, but I adjusted, singing louder to make sure I could be heard over him. We stumbled on, sounding like we were driving over a bumpy road until the song ended. When we finished, there was silence.

IN A JAM

"Okay, guys." Zane sighed through the intercom.
"Come up here."

I let myself breathe as Logan and I made our
way up to the booth. Logan had made a total mess
of my song. There was no way Zane would still want
us to perform together after that. He had to see that
teaming us up was a bad idea.

But the moment we walked in, Zane clapped
us both on the back.

"Great start!" he said to us.

Logan looked at Zane as if he'd just sprouted
a purple polka-dotted beard.

"Really?" I asked, wrinkling my nose.

"Yep!" Zane said, flashing a broad grin.

"Don't look so shocked," Portia added dryly.
"By the end of that round, the two of you sounded
great together."

I thought they both needed their hearing exam-
ined, but I knew better than to say that.

"Tenney, you look like you disagree," Zane said,
tilting his head.

"I just like the song better the way it was,"
I admitted.

"I don't," Portia said matter-of-factly. "Logan, the last beat you used was exactly what the song needs."

I gripped my guitar, trying to stay calm. I thought Portia was on my side!

"I guess I need some time to think about it," I finally managed to say.

"Let's wrap it up for today," Zane said kindly. "We'll meet again next Monday, but before that," he told us, "I want you two to get to know each other musically. The more you understand each other's musical influences, the better you'll be able to play together."

At Zane's request, Logan and I exchanged phone numbers. Then we said good-bye to Portia.

"I'm really looking forward to working with the two of you more," Zane said as he walked us out. I was still trying to figure out how to ask (nicely) if Logan and I had to work together when Zane turned on his heel and ambled back to the studio.

Logan stared out the front window at the parking lot while I tried to think of something to say.

"So...um...who are your favorite artists?" I said at last.

"There are too many to list," he said dismissively. "I'll text you a bunch of songs I like so you'll know what my sound is."

"Great," I said. I waited for Logan to ask me about my influences. Instead, he checked his phone.

"Well, I love singer-songwriters," I finally told him. "Paul Simon, Joni Mitchell, Taylor Swift . . ."

"I have to go," Logan said abruptly. He was looking past me, outside. A banged-up station wagon had just turned in to the parking lot. "See you," he said, and he ducked out the door.

On the drive home, I told Mom about everything that had happened.

"I can't believe I might have to perform with that kid," I groaned.

"It's just one performance," Mom reminded me. "It's not the end of the world."

"It sure feels like it," I muttered gloomily.

As Mom turned up our street, my phone chimed with a text.

"It's Logan," I said, checking it. "He sent me some songs as MP3s."

"At least he's reliable," Mom said.

I scrolled through the songs Logan had attached. Some were songs I knew, by Green Day and Bob Dylan. Some I didn't know. I clicked on one that I'd never heard of—"Tough as Nails," by a band called the Rusty Hammers.

As it started, crashing percussion made me jump out of my seat.

"Whoa!" I said, turning down my phone.

The song kept playing. It was more like a giant sound explosion than actual music.

"I know this song!" Mom said, her eyes lighting up. "The Rusty Hammers, right?"

"Mom, this is not a song," I protested. "This is a horrible musical accident!"

Mom laughed as I turned it off. "I don't think it's horrible," Mom said. "The Rusty Hammers were a local Nashville band back in the day. It's punk, ska, and bluegrass mixed with rock ..."

"And noise," I grumbled.

"I get it, you don't like it," Mom said with a laugh.

"I hate it! And it's one of Logan's favorite songs!" I said, letting out a sigh a mile long. "How are we supposed to find what we have in common musically if he has such terrible taste?"

"Honey, that seems a little extreme," Mom said. "'Tough as Nails' is an underground classic. A lot of people love that song."

"Well, it's totally different from the music I write," I griped.

"That is true," Mom said gently, "but if you listen with open ears, you can learn something from all kinds of music."

I squirmed a little. Of course, she was right, but thinking about being open to anything Logan had to say made me bristle.

"I don't like how he changed my song," I admitted as we pulled into our driveway.

"I get that," Mom said.

I looked over at her. "Is this how you felt when that producer tried to get you to dye your hair?" I asked.

She turned off the engine and faced me. "Honey, this is very different. Nobody is trying to change who you are or control how you sound. Zane and Portia are just trying to help you branch out as a songwriter. And Logan is adding to your song, not rewriting it."

She took my hands in hers. "It's your song," she continued, "but you need to be open. Collaboration is one of the most important parts of making music. It's what you create with other people that makes a song great. Whether other people are just listening or making changes, there's always going to be someone else involved. I know you're passionate about finding your own voice, but you need to let other people help you, too. Nine times out of ten, they'll make the music better."

I shrugged, twisting my seat belt.

"You know, when your dad first wrote 'Carolina Highway,' he thought it was going to be a foot stomper," Mom said, grinning. "But then I got my mitts on it."

I looked at her, surprised. "Carolina Highway" was my favorite song that Dad had written. It was a slow and bittersweet ballad, and I couldn't imagine it any other way.

"I thought Dad wrote it like that," I said.

"Nope," Mom said. "He was going to sing it himself as an upbeat bluegrass tune. When I heard it, though, I thought it sounded better slower, and in a minor key. We reworked parts of the melody together, too. Your dad would be the first one to tell you it's a better song now."

She ducked her head and looked me in the eye. "All I'm saying is, give Logan and his suggestions some time—he might surprise you." She smiled gently and climbed out of the truck.

I sat still for a moment as I watched her walk inside. I knew I needed to give Logan a chance. But a big part of me was scared about what would happen to my music if I did.

REALLY LISTEN

Chapter 7

*T*he next day, Jaya brought in a stack of flyers she'd designed for our book drive and showed them to Holliday and me. BOOKS FOR BANGLADESH! the flyer read in a splashy font. YOUR DONATIONS WILL HELP REBUILD A SCHOOL ON THE OTHER SIDE OF THE WORLD! In the center of the flyer, Jaya had drawn a beautiful illustration of a large book open to a photograph of Mina and some classmates standing in front of their school.

"Wow," I said. "It looks awesome! I only wish Mina could see it."

"Maybe she could," Holliday said. "Jaya, you should e-mail it to her."

"Great idea," Jaya replied, giving Holliday a high five. For a moment I felt sort of left out, but I told myself to shake it off.

REALLY LISTEN

When the final bell rang, Jaya, Holliday, and I roamed the halls, figuring out the best places to put them up.

"How about here?" Jaya asked, holding a flyer to the gymnasium door.

"Definitely," Holliday said. "Every kid in school uses the gym for PE, so everyone will see it!" Jaya held up the flyer, and I taped it to the door.

We worked our way down the hall, putting flyers on doors. As we did, I told them about my disastrous jam session with Logan. I was expecting Jaya to share my outrage, but instead she seemed confused.

"If Portia and Zane liked it, then maybe Logan's ideas are worth considering," she said, handing me another flyer.

"I have considered them," I said, frustration catching fire inside me. "But Logan doesn't care about my song, and he doesn't understand it. I'm not just going to let him come in and ruin my music."

"Who says he's going to ruin it?" Holliday asked.

"Yeah," added Jaya. "He might even make your song a little better!"

I stopped short. I wouldn't expect Holliday to

back me up—but Jaya? My patience snapped. "Never mind," I told her. "You can't really understand, because you don't play music."

Jaya looked like I'd just stepped on her toes. "Fine," she said quietly.

In a flash, my cheeks flushed hot with regret. I was about to apologize and explain what I'd meant when Holliday interrupted.

"We should ask other kids if they can help collect donated books," she said. "Charlie Wakida said he could collect from the senior center, and Tara Higgins said she'd do the post office and the grocery store."

Jaya turned away from me and focused on Holliday. "Good," she said. "The more volunteers we have, the more books we can collect and, hopefully, the more money we can raise."

Jaya and Holliday continued talking and planning as I quietly taped posters to classroom doors. Every now and then, I tried to find my way back into the conversation. But they just gave me halfhearted nods and kept talking with each other.

"We'll definitely need to work after school on the Friday before the Spring Clean," Holliday said.

REALLY LISTEN

"The event begins at ten o'clock the next morning, but I think we should get there early. Then we'll sell as many books as we can before things wrap up at two."

Jaya finally turned and looked directly at me. "Can you do all that, Tenney?" she asked.

"Yes," I said, a little surprised.

"I just know you're really busy with music," Jaya said.

"Right," Holliday agreed smugly.

"It's fine," I said firmly. "Of course I'll be there."

Aubrey and I were setting the table for dinner that night when a cymbal clash clattered through my phone. It was the sound I'd assigned to Logan's texts.

"That text alert is annoying," Mason said as he squeezed past Mom, who was dicing carrots by the stove.

"That's the point. It's from Logan," I said, checking my phone.

Aubrey craned her neck to see over my shoulder. "What did he send?"

"Another song," I said, squinting. On my phone screen was an MP3 link and a message: *So you can hear my vision.*

I frowned. "He didn't say what the song is," I said, clicking on the link.

The song started playing out of the phone's tinny speaker.

At first, all I could hear was percussion. Then a fuzzy guitar kicked in, and my stomach shuddered in horror as I recognized the melody.

It was my song.

I sat there, frozen, as Logan's growly voice came in, singing the first verse.

"I cannot believe this," I sputtered. "He changed everything, and he didn't ask permission first! It doesn't even sound like my song anymore."

For a moment, the four of us sat there, listening to Logan destroy my music.

"It actually sounds pretty good," Mason said. I shot him a cold glare.

Mason put up his hands in surrender. "I mean,

it doesn't sound like something you would write,"
he said, "but it's not bad."

"I have to agree, honey," Mom said.

I took a deep breath, trying to keep the fire rising
inside me from exploding. *Keep an open mind*, I told
myself—but it was impossible. The longer I listened
to the song, the angrier I got. When it ended, I was
burning with fury.

"Mom, can I call Portia?" I asked. "Please?"

Mom studied me. I knew she could tell I was
upset, because her voice was gentle when she spoke.
"Go ahead upstairs. We're eating at six," she said.
"I expect to see you back down here by the time
dinner's on the table."

I grabbed my phone and rushed up the stairs
two at a time, heading into my room for privacy. To
my relief, Portia answered after just a couple of rings.

"What happened?" she said when she heard the
panic in my voice.

"Logan happened!" I said, outraged. I told her
all about Logan recording my song.

"He didn't even ask! He just took my song and
did whatever he wanted to it," I said.

"It sounds like he's trying to help you hear what he's thinking," Portia said.

"I'd be more willing to listen if he weren't so rude," I said. "I can't work with someone like him."

"Tenney, musical collaboration isn't always about friendship," Portia replied. "You can make great songs with a person and not really like him or her, as long as you both respect the music."

"But Logan doesn't respect my music—he just wants to change it!" I said. "I don't want to share my song with someone who doesn't appreciate it. He's ruining everything."

"Take a deep breath," Portia said. "Your emotions are talking. Before you reject Logan's ideas, you need to take a step back from how you feel, open your ears, and really listen to what he's bringing to the song. And don't say you're doing that already," she continued, reading my mind. "Really listening means hearing somebody else's point of view. Do that, and you won't just learn about your song. You'll learn about yourself, too."

Portia's words echoed in my ears all through dinner. They echoed as I grabbed my guitar and songwriting journal and went upstairs. They echoed as I sat on my bed with my cell phone in front of me.

Really listen, I told myself. I tapped on Logan's text, getting ready to listen to his version of my song again.

Then my phone let out another cymbal crash. *What now?* I thought, clicking on the new text message. Logan had sent me a second MP3. *In case you want to sing along*, his text read.

I clicked on the link. After a moment, brisk drums started up. It sounded like the first track he had sent, but Logan's fuzzy guitar never came in.

It's an isolated drum track, I realized. Logan had recorded just the drums for my song, so I could use it to practice. *I guess I'd rather use this than listen to his voice and guitar ruining my song*, I told myself. I slid my guitar onto my lap and inhaled. Then I pressed play on Logan's drum track. As it started, I attacked the opening chords of the song on my guitar. I played through the song without singing. Instead, I tried to pay attention to how the mood of the song shifted when I played this way. It was angrier and bolder than the ballad I had originally written, but not entirely awful.

I played Logan's track again, this time putting down my guitar and singing along with the drums. I started the first verse and noticed how the fast, thundering beat made me sing louder, my voice taking on a rough edge. I listened to my lyrics and found myself growing angrier as I sang—angry at Holliday for coming between Jaya and me, angry at Jaya for getting Holliday involved in the first place, angry at myself for not being around more to help Jaya.

I'd barely gotten to the end of the first verse before I realized . . . I like this. It didn't really sound like my old song anymore. It sounded like something new.

I quickly restarted the track and picked up my guitar. I felt each note in my throat as I sang:

I thought I was the one who should be there
I thought it would be me
Got a taste of life's dish of unfair
You showed me clarity
You are the one by her side
While I'm here on the sideline

I moved into the chorus, and instead of listening for all the ways this version was different from the original version of my song, I just played, never quite sure where the song was going next. It was exhilarating. Logan's backbeat was always there, holding me up and pushing me to express how I really felt.

When the track ended, I took a deep breath. I felt like I'd just gotten off a roller coaster: I was emotionally exhausted, but also relieved somehow. Portia, Zane, and Logan had been right. *"Where You Are" is a rock song,* I realized. *A good one, too.* I couldn't believe I hadn't heard it before. And I couldn't wait to play it again.

UNEXPECTED HARMONY

Chapter 8

I was a little nervous when I showed up to rehearse with Logan on Monday after school. Although I'd worked a lot on "Where You Are" since Logan sent me his drum track, I wasn't sure how he'd react to the changes I wanted to make.

When I walked into the studio, Logan was already warming up at his drum kit, his arms and legs in constant motion. Watching him reminded me that there was a lot more to playing drums than just keeping a beat. You had to be able to do five different things at once while getting ready to do five more.

Seeing me, Logan stopped. "Hey," he said, out of breath.

"Hey," I replied. "Um ... is Portia here yet?" I wanted to talk to Logan alone.

"She just went to get some water," he said. "Zane and Ellie are going to join us at the end of the session."

"Oh," I said. My heart hammered against my ribs as I watched Logan thrash away at his drums. I was certain he had zero idea about the gyrations my stomach was doing as I got up the nerve to talk about my song. "So, I got your texts," I told him finally.

"Okay," he replied, twirling a drumstick between his fingers. It was hard to tell if he was nervous or showing off.

"I worked with your drum track for a long time," I continued, "and actually, I realized that your rhythm works really well for my song."

"Really?" Logan said curiously.

I nodded, and for a moment he looked as happy as a little kid. Then he caught himself and went back to acting too cool for school.

"Good," he said. "I'm glad you can admit you were wrong."

Ugh, I thought, irritation stinging me all over. I almost shot back something rude, but I stopped myself.

We sat there for a few minutes in awkward silence before Portia finally returned to the rehearsal room.

"Tenney!" she said, putting her hands on my shoulders. "How you feelin' today?"

I felt my cheeks redden as I thought about my freak-out the other night. "Much better, thank you," I said. "I spent the weekend working on the song, and I can see now that it's stronger at a faster tempo."

Portia nodded, satisfied. "Glad to hear it," she said.

I glanced over at Logan. "But I also have some ideas about how to make it even better," I said firmly.

"Great!" said Portia, handing me a bottled water. "We're eager to hear your thoughts, right, Logan?"

Logan nodded, but his eyes were guarded.

Focus on the music and be confident, I reminded myself.

"I like your backbeat," I told Logan, "but the tempo and melodic changes you made to the bridge were sort of . . . predictable."

Logan's mouth crimped into a frown, but I focused on my guitar.

"You did this," I said, playing Logan's version of the bridge. "I thought it might sound better like this." I strummed a new riff I'd come up with.

"I like it," Portia said. "It's similar, but more unexpected."

"What else?" Logan said.

"Well, there's the ending," I said. "I know it can't be soft and quiet like how I first wrote it, but right now it feels abrupt. What about something like this?" I said, playing my idea.

Portia spun her turquoise ring around her finger thoughtfully. "Mayyyybe . . ." she said. She gestured at my guitar, and I handed it over.

"What about playing a revised chorus to end?" she asked. "Something like this . . ." She played the last line of my verse melody, then launched into a riff on my chorus that built in energy and emotional power, then snapped to a stop at the end.

"I love it!" I said, clapping my hands.

"Yeah," Logan said, enthusiasm warming his voice. His eyes met mine, and he nodded. "This song is going to rock," he said.

"It already docs," Portia said, handing back my

guitar and grabbing a spare acoustic off the wall.

We worked through the song measure by measure, throwing out different musical ideas as we went. Some things we agreed on immediately; other things took a while. Even when the song changed to something I'd never imagined, I felt okay about it. I realized with a twinge of surprise that I was actually having fun working with Logan.

Once we'd worked through the whole song, we took a water break, just in time for Zane and Ellie's arrival at the studio.

"Well, it sure looks like y'all have found your groove," Zane said, tipping back his hat and surveying the smiling faces in the room. "Lemme hear what you've been working on."

Logan sat down behind the drums, I stretched my hands, and the two of us played the new and improved version of my song from beginning to end.

It was very different from what I'd first written, but I really liked playing it. All the way through, there were musical details that reminded me it was my song—the lyrics had stayed true to my real

feelings, and the melody was just a better version
of what I had dreamed up at school a few days
ago. The more we played it, the more fun I had.
After we'd finished a really boot-stomping performance of it, I couldn't help but grin. Ellie let out
a whoop of approval and applauded. Next to her,
Zane was grinning.

"Now *that's* the song it was meant to be!" he said,
patting me on the back.

Ellie nodded in agreement. "How do you feel
about it, Tenney?" she asked.

"I actually love it," I said, giggling.

"What's so funny?" Logan asked.

"Nothing," I said. "I just can't get over that new
ending. It sounds so good!"

"I know," Logan agreed. "Why didn't I think of
that?" he said, giving Portia a wink.

A broad smile spread across Portia's face. "I have
a feeling one of you would have come up with it if I
hadn't," she said.

Zane folded his arms with a satisfied look.
"See that?" he said. "I knew you two would make
a great team."

Logan caught my eye, and we exchanged a knowing glance. Working together hadn't been easy, but we had ended up with a great song. For the first time, I was glad that Zane had introduced me to Logan Everett.

DOUBLE-BOOKED

Chapter 9

*W*hen the session finally ended, we started packing up. I'd just snapped my guitar case shut when I looked up to find Logan in front of me, shifting from one foot to the other like he didn't know where to put either of them.

"Hey," he said. "I just wanted to say good job."

"You, too," I said. "Thanks for helping me make the song better."

"Well, you gave us great lyrics to work with," said Logan. I saw quiet respect in his eyes. "I think we work pretty well together," he said.

I wasn't sure how to reply, so I just nodded.

"Guys!" Ellie called to us. "Before I forget, we've got an update on the City Music Festival brunch."

The City Music Festival! I'd almost forgotten about it!

Zane clapped his hands together. "After today's rehearsal, I feel confident that if we work hard for the next few weeks, we can put together a set for you two to perform together that'll be a fantastic showcase," he said, looking from me to Logan. "The question is, are you both interested?"

Logan and I glanced at each other.

"Yes," I said boldly.

"Me, too," Logan said.

Zane slapped his thigh in delight. "Fantastic!" he said. "The festival starts the second week in April, and the brunch will be on the eighth."

My throat tightened all of a sudden.

"Wait," I said. "Isn't April eighth a Saturday?"

"Yes, ma'am," said Ellie.

My heart plunged. That day was the Magnolia Hills Spring Clean, when Jaya, Holliday, and I were supposed to host the book sale fund-raiser for Mina's school.

"What time does the brunch end?" I asked Ellie.

"Probably around one that afternoon," she replied.

The Spring Clean goes until two o'clock, I thought. If I moved fast, I could still make it to the end of the sale.

"Is that day a problem?" Zane asked, noticing my frown.

Playing at the artists' brunch for the City Music Festival was too amazing an opportunity to pass up. I couldn't face telling Zane and Ellie that I was trying to choose between the performance of a lifetime and a book sale.

"Nope," I replied. "I'll be there." I hoped that Jaya would understand.

Before school the next morning, I was a ball of nerves as I waited for Jaya by her locker. I finally spotted her coming down the hall, deep in conversation with Holliday Hayes.

"Hey, Tenney," Jaya said, gliding up. Without missing a beat, she started talking about the latest plans for the book drive. The more she talked, the more uncomfortable I got.

"And Holliday's dad is donating two hundred dollars to help meet our goal!" Jaya said exuberantly, beaming at Holliday.

"Wow," I said. "That's really great." I opened my mouth, about to ask Holliday if I could talk to Jaya alone, but I couldn't figure out how to say that without sounding rude. I snapped my mouth shut and swallowed hard.

"Are you okay, Tenney?" Holliday asked.

"Um, no. I mean, yes, but . . ." I took a deep breath, feeling heat rising from my neck to my hairline. "Something's come up, and I'm going to have to be late to the book sale," I finally blurted.

Jaya's eyes widened. "Why?" she asked.

I told Jaya and Holliday all about the City Music Festival artists' brunch performance and what a great opportunity it was—and finally that it was at the same time as the Spring Clean.

"I'll definitely be there for the end," I finished. "I just can't be there the whole time. Well, most of the time."

Jaya nodded and opened her locker. I couldn't see her face behind the locker door.

"I can still help collect books," I added weakly. "I'm really sorry."

Jaya shut her locker, hard. "It's fine," she said,

her voice sounding thin and strange.

"As soon as the performance is done, I'll come right over," I assured her.

"Whatever," Holliday said sharply. "You don't have to rush. Jaya and I have got it covered. Right, Jaya?"

I felt like my heart had just gotten stung by a bee.

Jaya looked up at Holliday and gave a half smile. "Yeah, sure. Don't worry about it, Tenney."

I put a hand on Jaya's shoulder and looked her in the eye. "I'll be there," I promised.

"Don't worry about it," Jaya said. "Look, I have to go ask Mr. Balcom about printing out more flyers. I'll see you in class."

Side by side, Jaya and Holliday walked away before I could say anything else.

FESTIVAL LIGHTS

Chapter 10

*T*he next few weeks rushed by like a river during the rainy season, overflowing with school, homework, rehearsals with Logan, and collecting books for the fund-raiser as I tried to show Jaya my dedication to our project. By the day before the Spring Clean, we had collected dozens of boxes full of used books to sell. Still, it was hard to know how much money we could actually raise to help Mina's school.

I spent my lunch hour pricing books in the school gym with Jaya, Holliday, and a few other kids who had offered to help.

"Do you really think this hardcover copy of *The Secret Garden* should only cost two dollars?" I asked, holding the book up.

Jaya pushed her rainbow headband back in her thick black hair and squinted at the book cover. "Yes," she said. "All fiction is two dollars apiece."

"But it's such a good book!" I protested. "I think we could sell it for more."

Holliday looked over from where she was sorting baby books. "I love *The Secret Garden*!" she said. "I bet we could get four dollars for it."

"You're probably right," Jaya said.

Holliday and Jaya exchanged an approving nod, and I suddenly felt very alone. Why did Jaya listen to Holliday when I had just suggested the same thing?

Jaya sighed, looking at the piles of books around us. "There's no way we're going to get prices on all these books by the end of lunch," she said. "I just hope we can finish by the time the Spring Clean starts tomorrow morning."

"We will," Holliday said. "We'll stay all afternoon if we have to."

I stared at the book in my hands, guilt creeping up inside me. "I'm sorry again about not being able to work after school," I told Jaya. "This afternoon's the last chance Logan and I have to rehearse before our performance tomorrow."

"I know," Jaya said quietly, but she didn't look

at me. She piled some books into her arms and carried them off to the bleachers.

Part of me felt as though I needed to apologize again, but another part of me didn't really know why I should have to. In the end, I just stood there.

"Don't worry about being busy, Tenney," Holliday said. "I can handle anything you can't."

I studied Holliday's face, certain she was trying to be mean. But her expression was oddly genuine.

"Um, thanks," I said, even though she'd just made me feel worse.

Holliday nodded. "Good luck," she said, sounding like she felt bad for me. Then she turned away and followed Jaya to the far end of the gym.

The next morning was a blur of getting up early and eating breakfast while Mom did my hair for my performance. Before I knew it, I was in Dad's truck, on my way to the City Music Festival artists' brunch. It was being held at a private home in Nashville's fanciest suburb, Belle Meade. Out the window, rolling

★ ★

FESTIVAL LIGHTS

green hills and wide stone mansions slipped past.

"How are you doing, Tenn?" Dad asked.

"I'm okay," I said, but my belly fluttered nervously. I wished my whole family could have come along to see me perform with Logan, but Zane had explained that it was a private event.

"Well, we're almost there," Dad said. "We'll even arrive a few minutes early."

The clock on the truck dashboard read 9:19 a.m. Jaya and Holliday had already been at school for twenty minutes, and people would arrive for the Spring Clean soon. As excited as I was about the concert, a big part of me wished I could be there for Jaya.

"Be ready to drive me back to East Nashville at one o'clock," I told Dad.

"How could I forget?" Dad teased. "You've already reminded me about a dozen times."

"Sorry," I said. "I just really need to be at school for the end of the Spring Clean. I promised Jaya I'd be there."

Dad nudged my jittering knee with his. "I know," he replied.

After a few minutes of silence, he squinted at
a driveway ahead. "I think this is it."

We turned off the road and stopped at a humun-
gous iron gate at least twenty feet tall.

"Ray and Tenney Grant," Dad said into the intercom, and the gate buzzed open.

He turned to me. "Are you ready?"

I nodded, inhaling deeply. Ahead, at the end of
a tree-lined driveway, stood a three-story mansion
the creamy-yellow color of eggnog.

"Wow," I breathed. With its tiled roof and turrets,
it looked like something out of a fairy tale.

"Who lives here?" I asked Dad.

"No idea," he said.

In front of the mansion, several glossy town
cars and a limousine with tinted windows sat
parked around a large circular fountain. People
in windbreakers with big cameras danced around
groups of nicely dressed guests, taking photographs.
As we pulled up, I spotted Ellie Cale with Logan
coming down the sweeping front steps.

Ellie wore sparkly cowboy boots and a bright
green sundress. Logan had on a collared shirt and

tie, nice jeans, and red sneakers. His hair had been combed into an old-fashioned rockabilly style, and he was twirling his drumsticks like crazy. Seeing me, he looked relieved.

"Hey," I said as I climbed out of the truck.

"Nice outfit," he replied.

"Thanks," I said, smoothing out the skirt of my floral dress and tapping the toes of my silvery boots. Mom had pulled my hair into a low ponytail so that it wouldn't bother me while I was playing.

I grabbed my guitar case from the backseat and said good-bye to Dad. "And don't forget—"

"One o'clock," Dad said, tapping his watch. "I'll be here. Now go ahead with Ellie! Good luck, honey."

I grinned and waved at my dad before following Ellie up the steps.

"They've set up a stage in the conservatory," Ellie said as we passed through the hulking front entrance into a marble lobby. "Logan's drums and the sound system have been set up and checked, and Belle's people said there's an office where you both can warm up before your performance."

"Who's Belle?" Logan asked.

"Belle Starr," Ellie said. "This is her house."

"Really?" I croaked as my mouth went dry. Belle Starr was one of the biggest singers in the world right now. It was exciting enough that I was standing in Belle Starr's house—but soon I would be playing my music here! My knees turned wobbly as I suddenly realized what a big deal this performance would be.

"Don't be nervous," Logan whispered, giving me a nudge.

"Too late," I whispered back.

We turned down a long hallway lined with windows. The sound of voices bubbled up as we reached a set of French doors halfway down the hall. Glancing through them, I gasped.

Inside, dozens of dressed-up people talked and laughed, swirling in a glittering sea among white tables heaped with flowers and food.

Zane came around a corner and spread his arms wide. "There they are," he said. "The stars of the show! You two ready for your big debut?"

"I think so," I said, nervously eyeing the crowd through the doors. "Where's the stage?"

FESTIVAL LIGHTS

"Up there," Zane said, pressing his finger to the glass. I followed his gaze across the room, where a drum kit and a microphone stood on a small platform between two ferns.

"Wow," said Logan, looking around the crowd. "There's Kit Harkins! He's my favorite guitarist! And look, Justine Gunn is here, too!"

"She is? Where?" I asked, pressing my nose to the glass. "My dad played her album nonstop last year!"

"Come on, you two," Ellie said, chuckling. "There will be plenty of time to stargaze once you're up on that stage."

We followed her and Zane into a small sitting room with rosebud wallpaper, pink-striped furniture, and a picture window framed in frilly curtains. Next to a little table holding a huge vase of lilies was a cluster of drum practice pads, which were like flat muffled drums; that's how Logan could loosen up his muscles and practice his beats without making a racket.

"Wow," Logan said, looking around the room a little skeptically. "This might be the floweriest room I've ever warmed up in."

"Well, get started," Zane said. "You two go on in less than an hour. Ellie and I have to go make sure everything's all set onstage. We'll be back soon."

Logan slipped behind the drum pads while I unpacked my guitar and started tuning, trying to calm the emotions storming inside me.

What if our performance doesn't go well? I thought as I twisted the E string peg over and over, tightening the string. I thought about my near-disastrous performance at the Bluebird Cafe a few months ago. I was so nervous and uncomfortable that I made a couple of false starts in front of the audience. But then I pulled myself together and played my song better than I ever had before.

Thwack! The E string snapped in two, hitting my hand and disrupting my train of thought. I growled in pain and frustration.

Logan paused his slow backbeat and raised an eyebrow.

"Geez," he said, as I started to change my broken string. "You're wound up tighter than that string."

"I am not," I said.

"Better loosen up before we get onstage," he

replied. "Unexpected stuff happens before a show. We just have to make it work."

"I know that," I said.

"Good," Logan said, speeding up his rhythm. "I wouldn't want you to blow this chance for us."

I turned away and rolled my eyes. Everything about him—his calm voice, his expression, the steady beat he was keeping—made me prickle with annoyance. I took my guitar and crossed the room to a door leading outside to the backyard.

"Where are you going?" Logan said, frowning, as I opened the door.

"I need some air," I said, and I slipped outside.

In the garden, I sat on a bench near a tall hedge and hugged my guitar to my chest. *I just have to make it through this performance,* I told myself, *and then I won't have to deal with Logan ever again.*

I took a deep breath and started warming up my vocal cords. "La-la-la-la-la-la-la," I sang. My voice was rough at first, but after a few minutes, it grew smooth and flexible, and I could easily hit both high and low notes.

Finally feeling calmer, I looked around. Ahead

of me, a curving cobblestone path stretched down the back of the mansion, surrounded by perfect rosebushes.

I pulled my guitar strap over my shoulder and began playing the intro to "Reach the Sky." I sang the first verse, my voice ringing out as the song carried me down the cobblestone path.

"Gonna be myself, nobody else. Gonna reach the sky if I only try," I crooned, the chorus lifting me out of my prickly mood.

I started the next verse and was rounding a corner of the enormous house when I nearly ran into a young woman who was looking down at her phone. When she looked up at me, I gasped.

It was Belle Starr.

Her porcelain features and long, sun-kissed blonde hair looked exactly as they did in the photos Aubrey had pinned up all over our bedroom.

"Oh! Hi!" I said a little too loudly, with an awkward half wave.

"Hi," Belle said carefully, like she thought I might be a crazy superfan.

"Sorry, I—I just . . . I was warming up for the

brunch and . . ." I stammered. I lifted up my guitar
to Belle, then realized she could already see it.

"Oh, you're one of the performers?" she asked.

I nodded until I remembered how to speak.
"I'm performing with Logan Everett, who's a drummer. We just started playing together, and I'm pretty
nervous, and I had no idea we were going to play
at your house . . ." It felt like my mouth was discon-
nected from my brain as I kept blabbering. "Anyway,
my sister's a huge fan of yours, and we have all your
records . . ." I ran out of breath, so I paused, sucking
in air.

Warmth crept into Belle's eyes. "Relax," she said.
"Take another breath."

I did, and then realized my mouth was hanging open. I snapped it shut and took a deep breath
through my nose. It helped.

"I didn't think I was actually going to meet you,"
I said.

"Well, here I am," Belle said lightly.

I grinned awkwardly, trying to ignore the fact
that my face felt like it was on fire. "I just want to say
thanks for letting us play here today," I said. "It means

so much to me, and I promise you'll enjoy it."

"Well, if it's anything like that song you were just playing, I'm sure it will be great," she said sweetly. "Good luck." With that, she slipped back inside the mansion.

I raced back to the room where Logan was warming up, feeling invincible. I'd just met Belle Starr! And she liked my song!

Logan frowned at me the second I walked in the door.

"Where've you been?" he asked.

Before I could reply, the door to the hall opened, and Ellie poked her head in.

"Guys, it's time," she said.

She led us down the hall to the conservatory, where the crowd seemed to have grown much denser. I struggled to keep up with Ellie and Logan as I edged past people with my guitar. At last, we made it to the stage.

"Break a leg," Ellie whispered.

With wobbly knees, I climbed up the steps to the stage. As Logan slipped behind his kit, I checked my mic stands. I use two microphones—one for my guitar and the other to sing into—and both had to be the exact right height. As I made adjustments, the crowd chatted in front of me. A few guests saw us getting ready to play and started making their way back to their tables, but most of them kept talking and laughing and paying absolutely no attention.

Zane stepped onto the stage and looked over at us with his eyebrows raised. "You ready?"

Logan glanced at me and gave me a crisp nod. "Ready," he whispered.

Zane switched on his cordless microphone. "Ladies and gentlemen," he said, his voice booming through the room. The crowd hushed, and people took their seats as Zane introduced himself and then Logan and me.

I looked out at the crowd. My stomach went into a nervous shudder. Nearly every person in this room had spent their life making music. They'd played all over the world, sold thousands of records, and won tons of awards. It was scary enough that Logan and I were about to perform for so many talented people. But the scariest thing was wondering what would happen if they didn't like our music.

OFF TEMPO

Chapter 11

"*P*lease give a warm welcome to Tenney Grant and Logan Everett!" Zane announced, spreading his arms wide. He hopped off the stage and gave us an encouraging thumbs-up.

The crowd clapped politely. I stood frozen at the microphone, my fingernails digging into my guitar like it was a lifeboat.

"Tenney!" Logan hissed. I looked over my shoulder at him. He leaned over his drum kit to me; his eyes were bright and fierce.

"Let's do this!" he said.

Logan's intensity woke me up somehow. Calm strength surged through me, and I nodded to him. *Yes. Let's DO this.*

"One-two-three-four!" Logan counted off, slapping his drumsticks together over his head, and we launched into the new song.

It only took me a moment to know that we were going too fast. Well, faster than we had rehearsed, anyway. As I scrambled to keep up with Logan, I checked the audience. They didn't seem to notice that anything was wrong. I shot Logan a warning glance over my shoulder, and he slowed down just a hair. My stomach relaxed, and I launched into the first verse.

"I thought I was the one that could be there. I thought it would be me," I sang. "Got a taste of life's dish of unfair. You showed me clarity."

I looked across the room. A few guests were bobbing their heads to the music. *They like it!* I thought. A jolt of excitement hit me, but I stayed steady, focusing on the next chords.

As we moved through the refrain, Logan and I started to click. His drums were like a heartbeat under my guitar, keeping the song alive.

I let my shoulders relax and finished out the chorus. "I see you've got it under control," I sang. "Just wish I could be the other hand to hold. I wish that I could be where you are, where you are."

My mind cleared as my lungs filled with pure

joy. We sailed through the next verse, the melody
from my guitar winding around Logan's backbeat. It
was like we were riding a bicycle together, each taking turns to steer. We sounded great . . .

. . . until we didn't.

As we started the intro to the bridge, Logan's
drums suddenly sounded like a jackhammer, too
hard and too loud. *What is he doing?!* I thought. I shot
him a glare, but he avoided eye contact, playing more
forcefully and intensely, as if he was the loudest
windup toy drummer in the world.

I had two choices: Match Logan's volume or
disappear behind his noise, and there was no way
I was going to let him drown me out.

I picked up my tempo, fingers leaping across my
guitar frets, and belted out the bridge. Logan's drumming got louder. Frustration tightened my throat, but
I swallowed it, pouring it into the song.

The drums throbbed in my ears. It felt as if
I was competing against Logan, not playing with
him. Still, I knew we needed to get through the
song. Fixing my eyes on a back wall, I breathed deep
from my belly and unleashed my voice for the final

chorus, fingerpicking notes down the guitar frets like wildfire.

> *I wish that I could be*
> *Where you are, where you are*
> *These words can only go*
> *Go so far, go so far*

We galloped through the rest of the song at a breakneck pace. Sometimes it felt like we were about to spin out of control and straight into a musical disaster. Instead, we swooped through the last reprise and landed at the song's end.

I closed my eyes, relieved I'd made it through, and applause hit my ears. When I glanced up, the mood had changed. Before, people had been distracted. Now, the room was electric, and a hundred pairs of eyes were on us.

"Thank you," I said into the microphone.

I scanned the audience as I tweaked my tuning for the next song. Zane stood at the edge of the crowd. When he gave me a big thumbs-up, I flushed with pride.

I glanced over my shoulder. Logan looked out of breath but pleased with himself.

"Ready?" I asked. Logan nodded.

"Try to keep up on the next one," he said, only half joking.

I rolled my eyes. *Logan may be talented*, I thought, *but I can't wait to get back to being a solo act.*

The rest of our set went fine. We played a few more of my songs, and covers of "Drive My Car" by the Beatles and "I Walk the Line" by Johnny Cash. Logan and I had rehearsed a lot, and we sounded good—and I realized I was actually having fun.

Our last tune was "Reach the Sky." When Logan and I had first started practicing together, I couldn't imagine the song working with percussion. Now, as the song unfolded, I could hear the depth that Logan's drums added to my melody, and I could feel him listening to me. When the song ended, we were perfectly in sync.

"Good job," I told him, under the applause.

He looked almost embarrassed, then shot me
a sideways grin. "You, too," he said.

Zane bounded up.

"Fantastic!" Zane yelped, pushing back his
porkpie hat in excitement. "The first one was a
bit bumpy at the beginning, but wow, Logan, you
really brought the heat to that one!" I smarted a
bit at that last comment but smiled as Zane turned
to me. "And, Tenney, those last three tunes were
phenomenal!"

"Thanks," I said. "Is there any water?" I asked.
My throat was parched.

Zane nodded. "At our table. This way."

He started moving through the crowd. As Logan
and I followed, though, guests kept stopping me
to congratulate us on our performance. Some were
concert promoters and label owners, and others were
musicians and singer-songwriters—I even had some
of their records! I wanted to ask each of them for
their autograph, but it seemed as though everyone
only wanted to know about us.

"Y'all are a pair of stars in the making," crowed
a man in a ten-gallon hat.

"Yes!" said a woman next to him. "Soon enough you'll be playing the Ryman main stage, breaking hearts and taking names." She winked at Logan, who turned beet red. Then she turned to me. "And how old are you, sweetheart?"

"Twelve," I replied.

She gasped like I'd just flown around the room. "Unbelievable," she said. "And you're signed at Mockingbird Records?"

"We manage Tenney and Logan," Zane chimed in firmly. "But they haven't been signed to a recording contract."

"Well, you'd better snap these two up before somebody else does!" the woman said, nudging Zane. Then she turned back to me and Logan. "How long have you two been playing together?"

"A few weeks," Logan replied.

The woman looked surprised. "So you're not a duo normally?"

I shook my head. "Just for today."

Ellie was straight ahead, waving to us by a table piled with pastries and fruit. I excused myself and pushed toward her with Logan at my heels.

"The set was good, right?" he said. "Even if I did have to save you on 'Where You Are.'"

I stopped dead in my tracks. "What are you talking about?" I said. "You didn't *save* me."

Logan snorted. "Tenney, we'd still be onstage playing that song if you had your way," he said. "That's how slow you were going."

"You were rushing!" I said hotly.

"No way!" Logan shot back. "I was just reading the crowd. If I hadn't picked up the pace, people would have fallen asleep in their seats!"

Heat rushed into my face so quickly I thought flames might shoot out of my ears. "I'm so tired of you doing whatever you want and then pretending like you did me a favor. You could have ruined my show!"

"Your show? You think I'm just here to make your songs sound better?" Logan said. "This is my show, too, you know."

I scoffed. "You wouldn't even be here if it weren't for me," I hissed.

Logan flinched as if I'd tried to hit him. "Yeah, right," he said, but I could tell that my words had shaken his confidence.

Before he could respond, I pushed through the crowd away from him. For a moment I stood there, lost among strangers. Then a voice broke into my thoughts.

"You look awfully serious for someone who just played a great set."

I looked up. Belle Starr stood before me. She flashed a brilliant smile.

"You really liked it?" I asked.

She nodded, and an excited squeak popped out of my mouth before I could stop it.

Belle laughed. "You guys have an awesome sound, and I love your voice," she said. "Do you write your own songs?"

I nodded. "I had a little extra help on that first song, though," I confessed, hoping she hadn't noticed how messy it had started. "We're still working out the kinks on that one."

Belle nodded and slid into a chair next to me. She took a muffin from the bread basket and ate a piece.

"Songwriting's tough, right?" Belle said to me. "It's such a great feeling when you write something good, but when you're stuck ..."

"It breaks your heart," I said without thinking.

"Exactly!" Belle agreed, her eyes bright with understanding. Suddenly, it felt like I'd known her for a long time.

"Can I ask you some questions?" I said.

"Sure," she said. "Ask me anything you want."

I'm not sure how long we talked, but it was a while. We talked about our favorite songs and our best and worst performances. I asked Belle how she got started in music. She told me about growing up in East Tennessee and learning guitar from her uncle Pip. She told me about getting discovered doing karaoke at a go-kart track and how she'd moved to Nashville once she'd signed her record deal.

"My mom came with me, but all the rest of my family and friends still live back home," Belle said.

"You must miss them," I said.

Belle nodded, resting her chin in her hand. "I love making music more than anything, but it can get lonely," she said quietly. "Can I give you some advice?"

I nodded and looked Belle in the eye.

"Keep your friends as close to your heart as your music," she said. "Even tiny successes are better when

you can share them with the people you care about
the most."

I nodded, my heart sinking as I thought of Jaya.
Jaya!

I pulled my cell phone out of my pocket to check
the time. My breath caught—it was a quarter past
one. I had five missed calls from Dad.

"Oh no," I said. "I'm sorry, Belle, but I have to go."

"Sure thing," Belle said. "But if you have any
more questions, Tenney, you can always e-mail me."
She handed me her card. "It might take me a little bit,
but I promise I'll write back."

"Really?" I said.

"Really," Belle said, her expression serious.
"I consider us friends now. And I always have time
for my friends."

With that, she squeezed my arm and slipped
back into the crowd. I felt like my fairy godmother
had just flown off, leaving me surrounded by her
magical glow.

The next few minutes were a blur. I grabbed my
guitar and thanked Zane and Ellie. Logan caught my
eye and I nodded a good-bye, but he just sneered and

looked away. I shook off my annoyance and ran
out to Dad's truck.

"Where've you been?" Dad asked. "I tried
calling—"

"I know," I interrupted. "Do you think we'll make
it to school before the Spring Clean ends at two?"

We looked at the clock on the dashboard. It was
one thirty.

"We can try," he said.

My lower lip quivered as I nodded. Inside, I was
flooded with guilt. How could I have forgotten to
check the time? I'd gotten completely distracted by
Belle Starr. I felt terrible.

Then we hit traffic, and I felt even worse. I texted
Jaya to say we were going to be late, but she didn't
respond. By the time we turned into the Magnolia
Hills parking lot, the clock read 2:23 p.m.

"Jaya might still be there," Dad said.

I jumped out of the truck and ran to the front
doors. They were all locked. Overhead, an orange
banner advertising the Spring Clean flapped in the
wind, taunting me.

I had missed Jaya's book sale.

A BREAK IN THE MUSIC

Chapter 12

I called Jaya's cell phone as soon as I got home. She didn't answer, so I left a message. Then I waited. And waited. I double-checked my text messages a dozen times. No response from Jaya.

"Just give her space," Mom said, squeezing my shoulder. "She's probably celebrating the fund-raiser with her family."

I nodded, but I was anxious. Jaya always texted me back right away, even when she was super busy.

I tried to keep myself occupied while I waited to hear from her. I restrung my banjo and sorted my guitar pick collection by color. I even answered every single one of Aubrey's bazillion questions about what it was like to meet Belle Starr. Her enthusiasm was infectious, and it helped me to share her excitement for a while—but Jaya was always at the back of my mind.

A BREAK IN THE MUSIC

By four o'clock, I couldn't wait any longer.
I needed to talk to Jaya face-to-face. I got permission
from my mom to walk over to Jaya's house and
grabbed Waylon's leash off the kitchen hook.

Jaya has to understand, I thought as Waylon
yanked me down the sidewalk. As sad as I was
that I had missed the book sale, performing at the
artists' brunch had been amazing. I'd met Belle and
performed in front of musicians and songwriters
who might want to work with me, and promoters
who could actually book me for real paying shows!
Jaya wouldn't hold that against me, would she?

Still, as Waylon and I walked up the drive to
Jaya's modern house, my stomach bunched up with
worry.

I knocked and waited for what seemed like an
excruciatingly long time. Then Jaya opened the door.
Seeing me, she locked her arms across her chest.

"Hi," she said in a flat voice.

"Hey," I said, trying to sound upbeat. "I know you
probably got my texts, but I just wanted to tell you that
I'm really sorry I ended up missing the book sale."

Jaya shrugged, her mouth scrunching into a frown.

"How did it go?" I asked.

"We made nine hundred and forty-two dollars," she said. "And that includes the two hundred dollars that Holliday's dad donated."

That was a lot less than the three thousand dollars that we had planned to raise for Mina's school. No wonder Jaya was upset.

"Charlie Wakida didn't show up, and Tara Higgins got the flu and had to stay home," Jaya continued. "We had too many books and not enough people to help."

"Oh no," I said. Now I felt even worse that I hadn't been there to help.

"Maybe we could do another sale to raise the rest of the money?" I suggested.

Jaya shook her head. "We already donated the books that didn't sell to Goodwill."

We stood there silently. I wasn't sure what to say. I was trying to think of another way we could raise money when Jaya spoke.

"How was your performance?" she asked, although it didn't sound like she really cared.

"Good!" I said. I told Jaya all about our set and

about meeting Belle Starr, hoping that it would cheer
her up.

As I talked, Jaya crouched down to pet Waylon,
like she wasn't even listening.

"Belle's really nice," I persisted. "We talked about
songwriting and performing, and she gave me tons
of advice—"

"That's great," Jaya interrupted. "I should go.
I have homework to finish," she said. She turned
away without meeting my eyes and started inside.

"I'm sorry you're mad at me," I blurted. "But
I did try to get there in time."

Jaya looked back at me. Her eyes were sharp.
"I just think you need to admit that things have
changed," she said.

"What do you mean?" I said, confused.

"Ever since you started playing professionally,
all you talk about is your new song or your next
show," Jaya replied.

"That's not true," I said.

"We said the fund-raiser was going to be our
project," she said, hardness creeping into her voice.
"Then you disappeared."

"Only after you brought Holliday in to replace me," I retorted.

"I needed help," she said forcefully. "I couldn't get you on the phone for more than a minute before you got distracted by whatever song was in your head that day. And as soon as you got a chance to perform somewhere, you forgot all about the book sale."

My temper rose inside me, but I kept my voice calm. "I didn't forget. I had to rehearse for a huge performance," I reminded her.

"Exactly! All you do is rehearse," Jaya shot back.

"Because it's important," I insisted.

"More important than Mina and her classmates?" Jaya asked.

I scoffed. "You know that's not what I meant. Today's performance was the most important show of my life."

"You always say that," Jaya said softly.

"Because it's true!" I insisted. "Every performance I do is important. Developing a musical career takes time and devotion."

"You know what else takes time and devotion, Tenney?" Jaya retorted. "Being a good friend."

I squinted at her, stunned. "It's not my fault that my show was the same day as your book sale," I said.

"You're right," Jaya said. "But it is your fault that you care more about music than you do about your friends."

Her words sliced into my heart. I was on the verge of tears, but I fought them back. "I'm sorry you feel that way," I said, as strongly as I could.

Jaya's mouth twisted into a sad knot. I thought she might apologize, but all she said was, "Me, too."

With a nod, I blinked back the tears pricking my eyes. Then I took off with Waylon down the driveway, leaving Jaya alone on her cold concrete steps.

AN UNEXPECTED ALLY

Chapter 13

*I*t's painful to be in a fight with your best friend, but it's agonizing to be in a fight when you go to the same school, are in the same homeroom, and sit next to each other in the same row—like Jaya and I do. From the minute I got to school on Monday, we couldn't avoid each other, and things were awkward. I spent first period staring at the back of Jaya's head, and when Ms. Carter assigned us to the same group for an activity, we both avoided speaking directly to each other.

Part of me wanted to tell her that I was sorry and let her know how much I valued her friendship. Another part wanted to tell her that if she didn't understand how important music was to me, then maybe we shouldn't be friends. The more I thought about it, the more my feelings melted into a confusing muddle, so I didn't say anything.

At lunch, Jaya ate with Holliday. I sat in the back of the cafeteria alone with my songwriting journal. I tried to write down how I felt, but my thoughts were like scattered leaves, blowing everywhere. Finally, I turned to where I'd started working on the lyrics for "Where You Are." The first page was covered with brainstorms and scrawled chord notes. Across from it, I'd written out the song's rough lyrics: two verses, a chorus, and a third verse.

The song stormed through my head as I read. The words had an angry edge, the way I'd felt after Jaya and I had argued. For a fleeting moment, I thought of Logan and the awful things we had said to each other at the brunch. I quickly pushed the memory out of my head. After all, I might never see Logan again. But Jaya was my best friend. Right now, all I felt was regret and loneliness, and a need to tell Jaya that she mattered to me.

Just then, a memory flashed in my mind of Mina telling us that her song was a prayer of hope for things to get better. I took a breath and turned to a clean page. My mind cleared, and a new lyric wafted into my head, fresh and bright. In a rush of inspiration, I poured my feelings about Jaya onto the page. As I wrote, my frustrations and sadness about our fight melted away.

When the bell rang at the end of the lunch hour, I felt a little better. But while working on my new song had helped me get out my emotions, I knew it hadn't fixed my problem. I still missed Jaya, and our friendship was still broken.

I needed some advice—and I knew there was only one person who could help.

At the end of the school day, my classmates rushed through the halls, eager to get outside and enjoy the sunny afternoon. I spotted Jaya walking with Holliday. They hugged good-bye before Jaya pushed through the doors to leave.

I squared my shoulders and sidled over to Holliday's locker right as she started spinning the combination lock.

"Hi, Tenney," she said, looking a bit surprised.

AN UNEXPECTED ALLY

"Hey," I replied. "Can I talk to you for a minute?"

Holliday nodded, opening her locker. Most kids at Magnolia Hills put a sticker or two on their locker doors, but Holliday had covered hers with glossy lavender wrapping paper with silver dots. I caught a glimpse of a miniature sparkly chandelier hanging inside. I couldn't help but admire it.

"Is this about your fight with Jaya?" Holliday asked.

I nodded. "Have you talked to her about it?"

"A little," Holliday admitted. "She's pretty mad at you."

I shifted awkwardly. It felt weird to be talking like this with Holliday. Sure, we'd worked together on the book drive and the Jamboree, but we had never talked about anything personal.

I think Holliday could tell I was uncomfortable, because when she looked at me, her eyes were gentle.

"I know how important your music is to you, Tenney," Holliday said carefully. "Jaya does, too. I just think she started to feel overlooked, like you didn't care about her or the book drive. Then when you didn't show up, it hurt her feelings."

"I know." I sighed, leaning against the locker beside me.

"Do you want me to talk to her for you?" she asked.

"You would do that?" I asked. "Why?"

Holliday twisted a golden curl of hair between her fingers, thinking. "Because I know how much your friendship means to Jaya," she said slowly. "It's true that we could have used more help at the book sale. But actually, if you had been there, it wouldn't have mattered to her as much that we didn't raise enough money. I think Jaya was so sad that you weren't there that her heart wasn't in it."

"Really?" I asked, sort of surprised. "I mean, you and Jaya seemed to be a pretty good team. I thought you didn't really need me, to be honest."

Holliday looked down at her sparkly sneakers, almost as if she was embarrassed. "You probably felt that way because I sort of took over—I know I do that sometimes."

Her mouth twisted, and for a split second, I thought she might cry. Instead, she took a big breath and lifted her eyes to meet my gaze straight on.

"I didn't mean to push you out," she told me. "I'm sorry for making you feel unimportant."

"That's okay," I said, realizing that Holliday was being sincere. "It wasn't really your fault. I could have tried harder to pitch in."

"Maybe it's not too late," Holliday said. "You should find a way to show Jaya what her friendship means to you."

She was right ... but how? Suddenly, an idea exploded in my brain.

"I know!" I said. "We still need nineteen hundred dollars for Mina's school. What if I raised it? I could save the school and prove to Jaya that I value our friendship at the same time!"

Holliday hesitated. "Tenney, nineteen hundred dollars is a lot of money ..."

"I could have a benefit concert at my dad's store," I exclaimed, the thought rushing into my head. "I could sell tickets and get someone great to play, like Portia!"

"True," Holliday admitted. Her eyes grew lively, and I could see the idea taking hold in her brain. "If

enough people showed up, we could actually reach
our goal."

"We?" I said.

Holliday hesitated. "I—I mean, I could help if
you wanted me to," she sputtered.

"Are you kidding?" I said, beaming at her.
"There's no way I could do this without you."

MAKING AMENDS

Chapter 14

"A benefit concert is such a great idea," Holliday declared as we walked out of the school. "Tenney, you have to perform! You're so talented, and this is a cause that means something to you."

"I don't know," I said uncertainly. "I don't want Jaya to think I only want to put on the concert so that I can perform."

Holliday put a hand on her hip. "Jaya cares about raising the money for Mina's school," she pointed out. "If you help to make that happen, she'll be thrilled."

I wasn't so sure. After all, raising the money for Mina's school had been Jaya's idea. I didn't want her to feel like I was taking the project away from her. In fact, I wanted the exact opposite—to show her that our hearts are in the same place. To do that, I needed to make peace with Jaya before I did anything else.

The next morning, I waited for Jaya by her locker. When she didn't show up, I went to find her in her favorite place: the art room. Our art teacher lets her hang out there before and after school to work on her own projects—and she usually goes there when she's upset or stressed out. I wasn't sure whether she'd be there, but I got lucky. When I walked in, she was hanging a freshly printed purple-and-yellow letterpress poster on a line to dry.

"Hey, Jaya," I said.

She looked at me, surprised. "Hi," she said. She moved to the art sink and started washing her hands.

"Can I talk to you for a second?" I asked.

Jaya dried her hands with a paper towel and looked at me expectantly.

"I just wanted to know if you could help me with something," I started. I saw a glimmer of interest in Jaya's eyes, but she didn't say anything. So I took a breath and told her about my conversation with Holliday and our idea for the benefit concert.

"I'm not sure if we can raise all the money we still need to repair the school, but at least we can try," I continued. "I told you how sorry I am that I couldn't make it to the book sale. Now I want to make it up to you."

Jaya's expression softened. "That's a lot of work," she said. "Do you really think you have time for that?"

"I'll make time," I said. "I know how important this is to you and your family. You and Holliday worked so hard—and I was just focused on my music."

Jaya looked down at the floor. "I never would have expected you to give up playing at the brunch, you know," she said.

"I know. But the truth is, I was being selfish," I admitted. "I should have helped out more with the book drive."

"I'm sorry, too," Jaya said. "The book drive was a lot of work, and when we didn't raise enough money I got really disappointed and angry—and I think I was just looking for someone to blame. It wasn't fair of me to expect you to care about this as much as I do."

"But I do care," I said, my voice catching in my throat.

Jaya's face broke into a wide smile. "I know—I can tell!" she said with a laugh. "I mean, you're planning a whole benefit concert to show it!"

"So you like the idea?" I asked.

"Are you kidding?" Jaya said. She came around the table and threw her arms around me. "I love it!"

As I hugged her back, it finally felt like things were right between us.

After school that day, I took Jaya and Holliday to my dad's shop to start planning. Once Dad and Mason were done ringing up some sales, I told them about our idea for the benefit concert.

"I thought we could do it two weekends from now, right here," I explained, pointing to the small stage at the front of the store. "I mean, as long as it's okay with you, Dad." I gave him my best pleading look and clasped my hands together.

Jaya and Holliday did the same right behind me.

"Please?" we all said sweetly.

"Well, how can I say no to that?" Dad asked
with a chuckle. "Besides, the store could always use
some extra publicity."

My friends and I jumped up and down in excitement, giving one another high fives.

"But if you really want this concert to happen in
a couple of weeks," Dad said, "we have a lot of things
to figure out."

Everyone started talking about plans at the
same time. It took less than a minute for me to feel
overwhelmed. There were a ton of details I hadn't
thought of, from advertising and bathrooms to how
many people the store could hold.

"I'd say you can fit about a hundred and twenty-
five people if we move all the records and music bins
to the storeroom," Dad said.

"How many tickets do you need to sell?" Mason
asked, watching me scribble down notes.

"As many as possible," Jaya chimed in. "We need
to raise nineteen hundred dollars for Mina's school."

Mason punched the numbers into a calculator
behind the counter. "Nineteen hundred dollars

divided by a hundred twenty-five tickets . . . they'll have to be about fifteen dollars per ticket."

Dad whistled. "That's pretty pricey for a benefit show," he said.

"That means we need to have music that's worth the price of admission," Holliday declared. She turned to me.

"You said you could ask Portia to play a set, right?" Holliday said. "That's a start."

"It is, but Portia can't be the only act," I replied. "Hey, maybe the Tri-Stars could play!"

Our family band hadn't performed in a few months, but to me this seemed like the perfect opportunity for the Tri-Stars to reunite. At least I thought that until I saw Mason shaking his head.

"No way!" Mason objected. "If I'm helping you run lights and audio, I can't play drums, too. I don't have four hands."

"We'll have to hold off on the Tri-Star reunion this time," Dad said. "But, Tenney, you should do a solo set."

I bit my lip and looked at Jaya, afraid that she'd think I was just looking for another excuse to perform.

To my surprise, her eyes lit up, and she clapped her hands together. "Of course!" Jaya exclaimed. "That would be perfect!"

"Okay, I'll do it!" I said. "I just wish we could have a real headliner."

The words weren't even out of my mouth before an idea struck me like a bolt of musical lightning.

"What about Belle Starr?" I said breathlessly. "She gave me her card when I met her at the artists' brunch. I could e-mail her and ask if she would perform!"

Holliday's eyes lit up. "Yes!" she exclaimed. "Don't forget that my dad is a vice president at her label. Maybe he could ask her manager!"

"This could totally happen!" I said.

Holliday let out an excited squeak, and I laughed. The more time Holliday and I spent together, the friendlier and more relaxed she had become. And now that I could tell she was a loyal friend to Jaya, I liked her even more.

"Seriously?" Mason asked, raising an eyebrow. "Belle Starr's one of the biggest acts in the world right now. She's probably booked for two years straight."

"Maybe, maybe not," Jaya said. "Sometimes people can surprise you." She flashed me a huge grin.

"Exactly," I said, smiling back. I thought how kind Belle had been to me when she gave me her business card. "I bet she'd want to help. We just have to let her know that it's for a good cause."

Dad let Jaya, Holliday, and me get on the laptop in the storeroom to e-mail Belle. It took us a while to figure out what we wanted to say, but after thirty minutes, we'd written something we all liked.

"Okay!" I said. "Fingers crossed something happens."

And as we all crossed our fingers, I clicked SEND. No matter what happened, I was glad that we were all in this together.

BANDING TOGETHER

Chapter 15

*T*he week raced by faster than a song in double time. Jaya, Holliday, and I spent every free minute planning the concert. Even with our parents helping and having the show at Dad's store, we were swamped with all the details. Every time we talked, we thought of something new to add to our to-do list.

During lunch on Friday, we met in the school library to continue working.

"I officially call this meeting to order," said Holliday, diving right in. "Silver Sun Records is letting us borrow a hundred and twenty-five folding chairs. My dad's going to have them delivered to Mr. Grant's store the day before the concert."

"Perfect," I said. "My mom's going to park her food truck outside the music store in case people want refreshments. And she's donating all the profits to Mina's school!"

"That's great!" said Jaya, looking up from her laptop. "What about our musical lineup? Have you heard back from Portia or Belle Starr?"

"Portia's in," I said, giving a thumbs-up. "As for Belle . . . when I checked my e-mail this morning, she hadn't written back yet. But I could check again now."

Jaya pushed her laptop across the table, and I signed into my e-mail account. I had one new e-mail . . . and it was from Belle! I let out a noise that was a cross between a peep and a squeak.

"She wrote back!" I squealed.

"No way!" Jaya said. "What did she say?"

I clicked on the e-mail and held my breath. When it popped up, I read it aloud:

Hi, Tenney!

Of course I remember you! Thank you so much for thinking of me for your benefit concert. It sounds like a great event and a fantastic cause.

I wish I could be there to perform, but I am on tour in Australia for the next three weeks.

*Send me all the details in case anything changes.
I hope the benefit goes well. It's great to see
that you're using your talent and your music to
make the world a better place.*

Your friend,

Belle

"So it's a no," I said. My heart felt like a popped balloon. Without Belle as the headliner, I wasn't sure our concert would raise enough money to rebuild Mina's school.

"That's okay, Tenney," Jaya said. "That just means you'll have to play a killer set!"

"No pressure," Holliday joked.

I laughed nervously. I had been so optimistic that Belle would perform that I hadn't given much thought to my own set.

"Do you know what you're going to play?" Jaya asked.

"I could play the songs that I performed at the artists' brunch," I thought aloud. "Except . . ." My voice trailed off, remembering the last time I saw Logan.

"Except what?" asked Holliday.

"Except I'd have to perform them without Logan," I said.

"So?" asked Jaya. "I thought you couldn't stand working with him!"

I shrugged, self-conscious all of a sudden.

"I know," I admitted. "But he's a really good drummer, and I sort of can't imagine playing some of those songs without him . . ." I could hardly believe the words coming out of my mouth.

"Then why not ask him to play with you at the benefit?" suggested Holliday.

"It's not that easy," I said, my nose crinkling with doubt. As I told my friends about the argument I'd had with Logan, I began to realize that my feelings about what he had said to me had changed. "Logan was really rude," I continued. "But I was wrong to make him feel like he didn't deserve to be there."

Jaya looked at me with solemn eyes. "If that's how you really feel, then you should talk to him about it."

I squirmed in my seat. Jaya was right, of

course. But even though I was ready to make peace, I had no idea how Logan felt ... or whether he'd ever consider performing with me again. I knew I needed to find out.

When school got out, I made my way to the front steps and pulled out my cell phone. *Maybe I should just text Logan*, I thought, but I doubted he'd reply. I knew I needed to talk to him face-to-face. So I called Ellie and asked her whether Logan would be rehearsing at Shake Rag Studios anytime soon.

"He's actually on his way here now to use a practice room," she said. "Should I tell him you called?"

"No, that's okay," I said. "Thanks, Ellie."

When Dad came to pick me up, I begged him to take me to see Logan at the studio.

"Tenney, I need to get back to the shop," he said. "Mason's there by himself with Aubrey."

"Mason's worked at the shop alone before," I persisted. "Please, Dad, I just need a few minutes. This is really important to me."

Dad sighed, but I could tell he knew I was serious. "I'll give you ten minutes when we get there," he said putting the truck into gear.

When we pulled up to the studio, I raced inside. By now I knew the maze-like hallways of Shake Rag Studios so well that I could find my way around with my eyes closed. I sped through the corridor and rounded one, two, three corners . . . and nearly slammed into Logan, who was coming the other way. He looked startled, then angry.

"What're you doing here?" he snapped.

"I came to talk to you," I said breathlessly.

He rolled his eyes and pulled open the door to the rehearsal room. I followed him in even though he hadn't invited me.

My stomach went into a nervous spiral, but Dad was waiting for me, so I just started talking. I told Logan about the girls' school in Bangladesh and Jaya and the book sale and my idea for the benefit concert.

"I was hoping that Belle Starr would play, but now it's just Portia and me," I finished. "And the more I thought about it, the more I realized

that my music sounds better when you're backing
me up."

"When I'm *backing* you up?" Logan huffed,
folding his arms.

"You know what I mean," I said. "We're a good
team onstage. We both need to listen to each other
more, but when we do listen, the music we make
together is great." I took a deep breath and launched
into my final argument. "Look, this benefit concert is
bigger than you or me or even Belle Starr. We have a
chance to help other people with our music. To make
a difference in the world. If you turn down this
chance, I think you're going to regret it."

"Really," Logan said.

"Yes, really," I said, trying to sound bolder than
I felt. "So are you in or are you out?"

Logan blinked. I had no idea what he was thinking until he spoke.

"I'll perform with you on two conditions," he
said.

"What?" I asked, breathing a sigh of relief.

"First off, don't ever say that I'm backing you
again," Logan said, looking me hard in the eye.

"Second, once the benefit concert is over, you and I will go back to playing solo. I don't need you to get me shows. And you can go back to writing your sappy songs on your own."

"Deal," I said, shaking his hand. "Believe me, nothing would make me happier."

A STAR ON THE RISE

Chapter 16

*T*he week leading up to the benefit was a blur of school, last-minute planning with Jaya and Holliday, and rehearsing with Logan. I came home every day exhausted, but still found the energy to do my homework, eat dinner with my family, and polish up my newest songs for the concert.

When the morning of the event finally arrived, I was ready. I woke up with a bolt of energy, got dressed, and zipped through breakfast. While my family was still finishing their grits and bacon, I packed up my guitar and put it by the door, eager to get the day started.

"Somebody's excited," Mason said, as he ambled over and started putting on his jacket.

"There's just so much to do!" I said. I snatched Dad's key ring off the wall.

TENNEY

Dad came over and plucked the keys out of my
hand. "Well then, we'd better get moving," he said.

"Let's go before Tenney self-destructs!" said
Mason, ruffling my hair.

"See y'all in a few hours!" Mom called from the
porch as we piled into Dad's truck. She and Aubrey
were planning to bring the food truck to Dad's shop
an hour before the show and sell snacks and refreshments before and during the concert.

"How are you doing, Tenney?" Dad asked as he
drove down Woodland Avenue.

I drummed my fingers on my knees as anticipation rippled through me. "I'm good. I just really
want this concert to be a success," I admitted, my
voice quiet under the hum of the truck's engine. The
moment I said that, worry pinched my stomach into
a knot. *What if after all this, we don't raise enough money
for Mina's school?* I wondered. I shoved the thought
out of my mind. I didn't have time to stress out. All
I could do was focus on what was in front of me.

We pulled into the parking lot behind Dad's
store. Holliday and her dad and Jaya and her mom
were waiting by the rear door.

"Hey!" Jaya grinned as I hopped out of the truck cab. Her arms were full of a big roll of blue fabric.

"Is that the banner?" I asked.

Jaya nodded. She'd designed a banner to hang above the stage during the concert. Holliday and I had helped her cut out felt birds and guitars for the last few days, but the overall design was a surprise, so I still didn't know what the finished product would look like.

"I can't wait to see it!" I said.

"You will," Jaya said with a sly smile. "But I'm guessing we have work to do first."

Jaya was right. The whole morning, the store swirled with activity as we moved all the furniture and bins to the storeroom and set up the chairs in rows in front of the stage. It felt like we had barely gotten started when Zane and Logan arrived outside the shop's front door.

"Sorry we're late," Zane said when I let them in.

"You are?" I said, checking the clock on the wall. It was almost eleven thirty. The concert was supposed to begin in just an hour and a half.

"We have so much left to do!" I said. "We need to

set up a ticket stand and get the cash box and—"

"My dad and I are handling all the money stuff," Holliday reminded me.

"Yeah, and my mom and I are dealing with the audience," said Jaya. "You need to focus on your music."

"Are you sure?" I asked.

"Yes!" they both exclaimed at once, and we all laughed.

"Thank you," I said, hugging them.

Logan and I went back to the listening room to warm up. Logan tapped triplets on his drum pad as I played scales on my guitar and warmed up my voice. After a while, we ran through a few songs. We didn't say much to each other, which I didn't mind.

I tried to stay focused on our performance ahead, but it was tough. I kept wondering how many people were going to come. Had we put up enough posters? A lot of our classmates had said they'd show up, but what if they didn't? *Maybe we should have sold tickets in advance*, I thought as my stomach sank. It's too late now.

Right as I started to feel like I could jump out
of my skin, there was a knock at the listening room
door. Portia poked her head inside.

"Howdy, whippersnappers," Portia said to us
as she came in. "Y'all ready for the big show?"

"Yes, ma'am," Logan replied. I just smiled
nervously.

Portia studied me and set down her guitar case.
"Tenney, you look about as cheery as a chicken on the
chopping block," she said.

"I just hope we sell some tickets, that's all," I said.

Portia let out a surprised guffaw. "Have you been
outside recently?" she asked.

I shook my head.

"Take a look," she said.

The moment Logan and I went out to the front
room, we saw what Portia was talking about. A crowd
was waiting outside Dad's store. I mean, a real
crowd. People clustered under the sign by the front
entrance in a line stretching beyond the length of
the store windows. I couldn't see where it ended.

"Whoa," I said under my breath. I'd never seen
so many people at Dad's store in my life. I looked

around. Zane and my dad were talking by the cash register, eyeing the crowd. Before I could ask them what was going on, Jaya and Holliday rushed up to Logan and me, both talking at once.

"Slow down," I said. "What's going on?"

"BELLE STARR!" they shrieked at the same time.

"She's here?" I asked, shocked.

"No!" Jaya said, breathless. "She posted about you online!"

Holliday whipped out her phone and stuck it in front of my face.

"Sad I won't be able to make a great show today @ 1 p.m. at Grant's Music and Collectibles in East Nash-ville," Holliday read out loud. *"Please go show your support for Patty Burns, Logan Everett, and my friend Tenney Grant! She's a star on the rise!"*

"A star on the rise!" Jaya squeaked.

"I can't believe it! Belle wrote that?" I squeaked. Was this really happening?

"Yes!" Holliday beamed. "And she didn't just write it, she posted it on all the big social media sites!"

"Belle's got more than three million followers!" Jaya said with an excited hop.

"Are they all going to show up?" I asked, feeling a twinge of panic.

"I don't think so," Holliday said, giggling, "but we are definitely going to sell out."

"Really?" I asked.

"Yes!" said Holliday. "There's more than three hundred people out there!"

I let out a spontaneous whoop of joy as Jaya, Holliday, and I high-fived.

"Dad, did you hear that?" I called to him.

"It's what Zane and I are discussing, honey," Dad said. His face looked pinched with worry.

"What's wrong?" I asked. Dad and Zane exchanged a glance.

"We have an issue," Zane said.

"It's great that so many people have shown up," Dad explained, "but we can't fit them all in the store. It would be a fire safety hazard."

I looked at Holliday and Jaya. All the enthusiasm was draining from their faces.

"But we can't turn people away now," I said. "Especially not after all this work."

"We might have to," Dad replied sadly.

Everyone started talking at once. As they did, I took a look around the shop.

And just like that, an idea cartwheeled into my brain.

"I know what we can do!" I exclaimed. "But we all have to work together—fast."

SINGING TO THE SKY

Chapter 17

"**W**hat's your idea?" Dad asked. Everyone's eyes were suddenly on me, like I was about to perform.

"What if we do the concert outside, in the shop's parking lot?" I asked. "There's enough room there."

"That's true," Dad agreed. "What do you guys think?"

"It could work," Mason said, "but we don't have much time to set up."

I looked around. Everyone nodded in agreement.

"Okay," Dad said. "Let's do this."

Usually, I spend the hour before a performance sitting quietly backstage, trying to stop being nervous. Not this time. During the last stretch before our concert, I felt like we'd been caught in a tornado. Aubrey, Logan, Jaya, Holliday, and I shuttled drums, gear, chairs, and cables out to the parking lot. Dad and Zane helped Mason reset the sound system as Holliday's dad and Jaya's mom strung Jaya's banner over the space where we'd set up our makeshift outdoor stage.

"Wow," I breathed, as the navy fabric unfurled and scrolling white letters became clear. MUSIC HELPS THE WORLD, it read. Songbirds, musical notes, and tiny globes danced around the words on a background that glittered like a starry sky.

"It's beautiful!" I told Jaya.

"Well, I was inspired," Jaya said happily.

With less than twenty minutes before the concert was scheduled to start, we were ready. Well, almost.

"You're going to go onstage looking like that?" Aubrey said, squinting at me.

"Thanks a lot," I said, but as I wiped sweat off my face and looked down at my grass-stained jeans, I knew she had a point.

Aubrey ran to get Mom, who came to my rescue with a duffel bag of emergency items.

As we hustled back to the storeroom to get me cleaned up, I turned to Mom. "Are you sure you don't need to be in the food truck?" I asked.

SINGING TO THE SKY

Mom nodded. "We sold out of everything!" she said. "Besides, the crowd is gathered in front of the stage. No one's thinking about food anymore. They want to hear some music!"

She quickly ran a brush through my hair as Aubrey set out a fresh outfit that she'd picked just for me: a pretty chambray shirt, white lace shorts, and a floppy felt hat.

"I packed you an outfit at the last minute because I thought you might need it," Aubrey said confidently. Ever since she helped me get dressed for my show at the Bluebird Cafe, my little sister liked to think of herself as my personal stylist.

I rolled my eyes good-naturedly. "Thanks for looking out for me, Aubrey," I said, slipping on the new outfit.

Through the walls, I could hear the steady rumble of voices and bodies shifting in the parking lot.

"I wonder how many people are out there," I said anxiously.

"Don't worry about that now, sweetheart," Mom replied, shaking her head. "All that matters is that you give them a great show, right?"

I nodded, and she wrapped me in a hug.

"You focus on the music and let the rest take care of itself," she whispered in my ear.

A knock sounded on the storeroom door. I opened the door and found Logan behind it. From his nervous expression, I could tell it was time to go on. Slinging my guitar across my shoulders, I followed him down the hall to the back door. Bright sunlight blinded me as we walked out. Then I saw the crowd filling the whole parking lot right up to the stage. I recognized some kids from school and a few regular store customers, but most of the faces were ones I'd never seen before.

I spotted Jaya, who had agreed to emcee, standing next to the stage. Seeing us, her eyes lit up. "Ready?" she mouthed.

Logan and I nodded. In a heartbeat, Jaya hopped onstage and over to the lead microphone.

"Y'all ready to hear some great music?" she asked energetically. The crowd erupted into applause. "Thank you all for coming to support a cause that's very close to my heart," said Jaya. "The money you've given today will help to rebuild my cousin's school in Bangladesh."

I looked into the crowd and saw people's faces
light up as Jaya continued. "As you know, our opening
act has some big fans here in Nashville . . . and you're
about to find out why. Please welcome Logan Everett
and my best friend, Tenney Grant!"

My stomach was a cluster of butterflies as
Logan and I waded through the crowd to the stage.
The moment I stepped behind the microphone and
swung my guitar into position, though, I felt rooted
and alive, like I was home.

"Hi there," I said into the microphone. "We're so
excited to be with y'all today and play our music."

I flashed a look at Logan. He was watching me,
drumsticks up, waiting for his cue.

"One-two-three-four!" I counted off, and we
jumped into our first song, "Reach the Sky." It's spir-
ited and passionate, and we'd figured a few people
might have seen the online video of me playing it at
the Jamboree with Portia. Sure enough, it got a lively
response. The whole crowd clapped to the beat. I even
heard a few voices singing along. It felt amazing!

After it ended, we went right into another of my
songs, "Good Morning, Glory." A few times, Logan's

tempo started to race. When that happened, I'd shoot a glance at him and he'd pull back. *I hear you*, his eyes told me. By the time we played the fourth and fifth songs, we didn't even have to look at each other to communicate. It was as if we both could feel what the other one was doing—like we were speaking to each other through the music.

When that song ended, it was Logan's turn to count off.

"One-two-three-four!" he shouted, then exploded into the driving beat for "Where You Are." I came in after a measure, matching his fire.

I thought I was the one who should be there
I thought it would be me
Got a taste of life's dish of unfair
You showed me clarity
You are the one by her side
While I'm here on the sideline

I looked down into the crowd and saw Holliday looking up at me. Did she realize that the song was about her? I pressed forward, looking her in the eye

and urging her to keep listening. When we got to the
bridge, I sang a new set of lyrics that I wrote right after
I realized what a good friend Holliday could be.

> *I've been so out of touch lately*
> *Been caught up with myself*
> *Been taking out my anger on somebody else*
> *I'm so sorry*
> *I know you don't mean me any harm*
> *You're just being a good, good friend*
> *Making light of the dark*

Holliday grinned, clapping along as I sang the
final chorus.

> *I just want to be*
> *Where you are, where you are*
> *These words can only go*
> *Go so far, go so far*
> *So now we have worked it all out*
> *Thank you for erasing my doubt*
> *I just want to be*
> *Where you are, where you are*

Finally, Logan and I snapped the song to a sharp
finish. The crowd burst into cheers before I could
even breathe.

"Thank you," I said, over the applause. I looked
at Logan. He was grinning at me, his eyes aflame.
I told you we could do it, his look seemed tell me. I
smiled back, telling him I knew he was right.

As I finally took a breath, the crowd grew quiet.

"This next song is our last one," I continued.
There were a few scattered boos, which made me
smile. I looked over at Logan, knowing that he had
expected "Where You Are" to be our last song. He
pressed his lips into a thin line.

"Just listen," I whispered. "And join in whenever
you're ready."

I turned back to the crowd and scanned the faces
until I found Jaya again. She was standing where she'd
been from the very beginning, beaming.

"I wrote this song for my best friend, Jaya,"
I told the crowd, "because she believes in helping
people more than anyone I know. Working with
her on this project, I've learned something very
important—everything gets better when you share

it. Like friendship, music doesn't just make you feel better," I said, talking right to Jaya, "it makes the world a better place. This is called 'Music in Me.'"

I looked down at my guitar. The songbird above the strings sparkled in the sunlight, like it could fly away. I took a deep breath and started playing.

"You put your life in my dreams," I sang, "and help things go right behind the scenes. You mean so much to me. And I hope you see . . ."

Logan started a slow, steady beat as I sang the chorus:

Every time I play
You're the music, you're the music
In every word I sing
You're the music, you're the music
You are the music in me

We started the bridge, and my fingers danced across my guitar's frets. "You'll be by my side so don't be afraid," I sang. "I'd rather say I tried than let this dream fade."

Jaya was glowing as she listened to my words.

I smiled at her, and when she smiled back, my heart
swelled with happiness.

When the song ended, a wave of wild applause
hit us. Logan and I bowed and shared a grin. As Zane
took the stage to introduce Portia, we started offstage.

"That was pretty great," Logan said, his eyes
bright. "I know I said that your songs are sappy, but
that new one was actually not half bad."

"Thanks, I guess," I said. "I liked the drums you
added."

He smiled, but before we could say anything
else, we were bombarded by fans asking for selfies
and autographs.

Portia strummed the opening chords to her first
song, and the audience grew quiet. I looked through
the crowd. Between strangers, I spotted my family,
Holliday, Jaya, and their parents. Everyone was sway-
ing to the music, as if they shared the same heart.
I looked up to the sky. As we sang along to Portia's
song together, I could feel the world getting brighter.

NEXT STEPS

Chapter 18

*T*he next weekend, Jaya and I invited Holliday to join us for our "breakfast-for-dinner" sleepover. Mom made biscuits, grits, bacon and eggs, fresh fruit salad, and my favorite blueberry muffins with brown-sugar tops.

"Thank you so much for making all this, Mrs. Grant," Holliday said, spreading blackberry jam on her last bite of biscuit.

"Well, I thought you three deserved a reward for working so hard on the concert," Mom replied. "How much did y'all end up raising in the end?"

"Our final tally was over five thousand dollars," Jaya said proudly. "My mom wired the money to Bangladesh on Monday. They've already started repairing the school!"

"I can't wait to see photos when it's done," I said.

Jaya looked at me, her eyes flickering with mischief. "That reminds me, can I use your laptop, Tenney?" she asked, jumping up. "I want to show you something cool."

I grabbed my laptop from the family room. We booted it up at the kitchen table and clustered around it.

"What is it?" I asked, as Jaya quickly navigated to her e-mail.

"A surprise," she trilled. She selected a message from her cousin Mina and read it aloud:

Dear Jaya, Tenney, and Holliday,

Thank you so much for the amazing work you did to help my school. The money you raised covered more than just the repairs on our school building—it also made it possible for us to hold our school concert on time! Our music teacher, Miss Alimah, my friends, and I want to thank you for everything. I hope you enjoy the video!

Love, Mina

Jaya clicked on the attachment, and a video

started playing. Mina and a group of her friends
in white-and-navy school uniforms stood in a
half circle in front of the camera with their instruments. Their teacher, who I guessed was Miss
Alimah, stood off to the side. She raised her hands,
and Mina and her friends got their instruments
into position.

"What are they doing?" I asked.

"You'll see," Jaya said with a wink.

Miss Alimah signaled to Mina, who held up
her *esraj* and ran her bow over the strings, playing
a familiar melody. As her friends joined in on their
instruments, I realized they were playing the song
I wrote for Jaya.

"You put your life in my dreams and help things
go right behind the scenes," they sang. "You mean so
much to me. And I hope you see that every time
I play, you're the music . . ."

Hearing the girls sing my words, I felt strange
but amazing, like I was in a beautiful dream.

Jaya noticed that I had tears in my eyes. "Are you
okay?" she asked.

I managed a nod. As the girls kept singing, my

heart felt like it was overflowing with joy.

"That was incredible," I said once the video had finished. "But how did they know the song?"

"Mom recorded your performance with Logan," Jaya said, "and we e-mailed it so that Mina and her friends could see the concert, too."

"Thank you, Jaya," I said.

Jaya shook her head. "We should thank you," she said.

Holliday nodded. "Tenney, if it weren't for you, none of this would have happened."

"If it weren't for us," I said. And as the three of us shared a smile, I realized that to me, one of the only things more powerful than music was friendship.

A few days later, Zane called and asked me to come down to meet with him at his office.

"Maybe he wants to talk to me about the song I wrote for Jaya," I said to Mom as we drove downtown to Music Row.

NEXT STEPS

"Could be," Mom said, but her eyes flashed in a way that made me suspect that she knew more than she was letting on.

The moment we sat down to talk, I showed Zane the video of Mina and her friends singing "Music in Me." When it was over, Zane gave a low whistle of approval.

"Not too shabby," he said, tipping his porkpie hat back on his head like he does when he's impressed. "So how did it feel, hearing other people sing your song?"

"It was strange at first," I admitted. "But then I loved it!"

"Yes," Zane agreed. "When someone loves your songwriting, it's the best feeling in the world," he said, and we shared a smile.

"In any case," he said, "it's something you're going to have to get used to, because you are very talented, Tenney. You've got so many songs in you that people are going to love."

"I hope so," I said, as heat flooded my face.

"Well, I know so," Zane continued. He leveled his gaze at me, his face serious. "Tenney, we've been working together for a few months now, and in that time I've watched you take on every challenge without hesitation." He paused, and a smile lit up his face. "Well, maybe Logan threw you a few curveballs that you tried to duck, but in the end you were pitching 'em right back."

Hearing Logan's name made me squirm in my seat. I tried to change the subject. "Do you think I'll get another chance to perform soon?"

"Well, ever since Belle Starr tweeted about you and your benefit concert, I've been getting a lot of interest in bookings," Zane told me. "Now that you've got a solid performance set, I think we need to start scheduling small shows."

"Really?" I asked. "That's great! I love my new songs that I've written with you and Portia."

"So do we," said Zane. "In fact, I like them so much that I'd like to officially sign you to a recording contract."

My spine went numb as pure excitement charged through me. When I looked at Mom, she gave me a knowing smile.

"Wait, you knew about this?" I asked her.

She nodded. "Zane pulled your father and me aside after your performance and asked our permission."

"And you waited a whole week to tell me?" I exclaimed.

Mom laughed. "Your dad and I wanted a little time to review the contract and talk with a lawyer about what you are committing to," she said. "Besides, we thought Zane should be the one to tell you."

With a gentle smile, Zane slid a folder and a pen across the desk. "So what do you say, Tenney. Would you like to sign with Mockingbird Records?"

"Yes!" I said, grabbing the pen.

"You're the whole package, Tenney," Zane said, opening the folder and pulling out my contract. "I want you to take your time and develop as an artist and a songwriter. At this rate, I can see you guys being ready to record in less than two years."

"W-wait," I stammered. "You . . . guys?" I felt my breath freeze in my chest.

"Yeah, you and Logan!" Zane said enthusiastically. He leaned toward me, eyes bright. "You two are great together. When your set ended at the benefit show, I knew you two were going to be huge!"

You two. As in Logan and me. Performing as
a duo. Permanently.

My brain felt like it had just been thrown into
a blender. I realized I had no idea what to do.

Logan and I made a deal never to work together again,
I thought. *Maybe he'll refuse to sign, and Zane will offer
me a solo contract.*

The words swam around on the page as I stared
at the contract.

"Don't worry, honey," Mom said. "Dad and I
have already read all the fine print on everything.
Your music is protected."

"Absolutely," Zane agreed.

I nodded, scanning the contract. The typing was
dense, and it was several pages long, but at the bottom
of the fourth page, I found the signature lines . . . and
gasped. I could hardly believe it—Logan had signed
on his line in sharp, blocky letters.

"What do you think?" Zane asked me.

I opened my mouth, then closed it again. For the
first time in a very long while, I had no idea what to
say. Then Logan's face flashed in my memory, bright

with pride, the way he'd looked at the end of our benefit show.

Maybe being in a duo with Logan won't be so bad, I told myself. *After all, no matter what, Logan loves music as much as I do. That's the most important thing.*

"Tenney, are you okay?" Mom asked.

"Yes," I told her.

Then I put the pen to the page and signed my name.

SONG LYRICS

Music in Me

by Kate Cosentino

You put your life in my dreams
And help things go right behind the scenes
You mean so much to me
And I hope you see

Chorus:
That every time I play
You're the music, you're the music
In every word I sing
You're the music, you're the music
You are the music in me

When I look at the crowd
Your smiling face stands out
You taught me this is what life's all about
So I hope I make you proud

'Cause every time I play
You're the music, you're the music
In every word I sing
You're the music, you're the music
You are the music in me

Bridge:
You'll be by my side
So don't be afraid
I'd rather say I tried
Than let this dream fade

Every time I play
You're the music, you're the music
In every word I sing
You're the music, you're the music
You are the music in me

Where You Are

by Ashley Leone

I thought I was the one who should be there
I thought it would be me
Got a taste of life's dish of unfair
You showed me clarity
You are the one by her side
While I'm here on the sideline

Chorus:
I wish that I could be
Where you are, where you are
These words can only go
Go so far, go so far
I see you've got it under control
Just wish I could be the other hand to hold
I wish that I could be
Where you are, where you are

It was only going to be her and me
And then you came in with your thoughts
Planning everything so perfectly
Giving your best shot
Now while I'm over here alone
You're making sure she isn't on her own

I wish that I could be
Where you are, where you are
These words can only go
Go so far, go so far
I see you've got it under control
Just wish I could be the other hand to hold
I wish that I could be
Where you are, where you are

Bridge:
I've been so out of touch lately
Been caught up with myself
Been taking out my anger on somebody else
I'm so sorry
I know you don't mean me any harm
You're just being a good, good friend
Making light of the dark

I just want to be
Where you are, where you are
These words can only go
Go so far, go so far
So now we have worked it all out
Thank you for erasing my doubt
I just want to be
Where you are, where you are

ABOUT THE SONGWRITERS

KATE COSENTINO began playing the guitar and singing when she was six years old and wrote her first song at the age of ten, just like Tenney. Now seventeen, Kate is inspired by everything around her, writing songs about subjects ranging from Batman to the periodic table of elements.

Kate loves performing her songs onstage, and she dreams of moving the world with her music. She loves when people tell her that they relate to her song lyrics, because she sees music as a tool to comfort others and make people feel connected.

While writing the song "Music in Me," Kate thought about what it was like for her as a young songwriter trying to find her voice as a musician. Like Tenney, Kate faced some disappointments, but she learned that the most important thing is to "always say yes to yourself. I believe in my music and I like it, and that's what matters in the first place." If other people like it, too, she adds, that's just icing on the cake.

ASHLEY LEONE is a singer-songwriter from Blue Bell, Pennsylvania. Ashley always knew that she wanted a life in music, but she knew she'd have to overcome her shyness first.

She used to sing so quietly that she auditioned for her middle school choir three times before she earned a spot. Ashley was very nervous when she sang her first solo, but it helped her gain the confidence to start singing live in front of an audience. In high school, she began performing at open mics and earned a few acoustic shows, which led to opportunities at bigger venues with a band backing her up. Ashley says that when she performs, she takes on a different persona that is more confident and more true to herself.

Ashley enjoyed trying on yet another persona when she wrote the song "Where You Are" for Tenney. As a young songwriter and big fan of American Girl, Ashley felt a deep connection with Tenney's go-getter attitude and the challenges she faced trying to balance her music career with her personal life. "Being a musician myself, I understand how Tenney feels when she can't always be there for things," Ashley says. "So this song definitely touches me."

SPECIAL THANKS

With gratitude to manuscript consultant
Erika Wollam Nichols for her insights and
knowledge of Nashville's music industry;
to music director Denise Stiff for guiding
song development; and to songwriters
Kate Cosentino and Ashley Leone
for making Tenney's story sing.

ABOUT THE AUTHOR

As a young reader, Kellen Hertz loved L. Frank Baum's Wizard of Oz series. But since the job of Princess of Oz was already taken, she decided to become an author. Alas, her unfinished first novel was lost in a sea of library books on the floor of her room, forcing her to seek other employment. Since then Kellen has worked as a screenwriter, television producer, bookseller, and congressional staffer. She made her triumphant return to novel writing when she coauthored *Lea and Camila* with Lisa Yee before diving into the Tenney series for American Girl. Kellen lives with her husband and their son in Los Angeles.

Request a FREE catalog at
americangirl.com/catalog

Sign up at **americangirl.com/email**
to receive the latest news and exclusive offers

READY FOR AN ENCORE?

VISIT

americangirl.com

for Tenney's world

OF BOOKS, APPS,

GAMES, QUIZZES,

activities,

AND MORE!